The Gentle Scholar

The Gentle Scholar

The Forgotten Story of
JOHN M. WEBB
and the
Webb School
in
Bell Buckle, Tennessee

TERRY BARKLEY

BRAYBREE
Publishing

Copyright © 2015 Terry Barkley
All rights reserved

Published by BrayBree Publishing Company LLC
FIRST EDITION

No part of this book may be reproduced, stored in or introduced into a retrieval system or transmitted in any form or by any means (electronic, mechanical, photocopying, recording, or otherwise) without the prior written permission of the publisher and copyright owner.

The scanning, uploading, and distribution of this book on the Internet or through any other means is not permitted without permission from the publisher and copyright owner.

ISBN-13: 978-1-940127-10-1

Printed in the United States of America

BRAY BREE BrayBree Publishing Company LLC
P.O. Box 1204
Dickson, Tennessee 37056-1204

Visit our website at www.braybreepublishing.com

*In loving memory of my mother, Violet (Taylor) Barkley (1923–2005),
my brother J.R., Hillard R. Barkley Jr. (1947–2010)
and my great friend, John L. Heatwole (1948–2006).*

ACKNOWLEDGEMENTS

A host of people have contributed to this work—no researcher and writer can do this type of work alone—and I wish to formally thank them at this time for their contributions. I also apologize in advance for any glaring omissions.

First, I thank Margaret (Maggi) Britton Vaughn, Bell Buckle's Poet Laureate of Tennessee, for her wonderful foreword to this book. Maggi also served as a critical reader of the manuscript, as did Vietnam veteran Glenn N. Holliman of Newport, Pennsylvania, a former administrator and history teacher at The Webb School in Bell Buckle, and one well-versed in the school's history. Their comments and suggestions for improving this work are greatly appreciated.

My friend and former colleague at Marion Military Institute, KellyAnn Griffiths, worked her "magic" on the entire project, providing me with a clean, presentable manuscript to offer prospective publishers.

The former director of the Baer Memorial Library at MMI, KellyAnn is presently the electronic resources librarian and assistant director of the library at Shelton State Community College in Tuscaloosa, Alabama.

At The Webb School itself, a number of administrators, faculty, and staff—past and present—have contributed to this project over the years including the redoubtable Dorothy P. Elkins in the alumni and development office; former Headmaster Jackson E. Heffner; former Assistant Headmaster Del R. Coggins; former Librarian Sandy Sanders; former Headmaster A. John Frere and his wife, Penny; Kimi Abernathy; historian and master teacher, L. R. Smith; Richard Miller; and Matthew Wilson, Director of Annual Giving and Alumni Relations. A very special thank you goes to Hannah Byrd Little, Library Director of the William Bond Library at Webb, and to Susan Coop Howell, Archivist and Librarian's Assistant, who facilitated my successful research visits and who always went the extra mile in answering my many inquiries. These ladies are the keepers of the school's past, and both are wonderful assets to The Webb School.

In the village of Bell Buckle itself, Maggi Vaughn and Billy Phillips (Phillips General Store) proved most helpful.

Data and an image regarding the John Webb home on Maple Street in Bell Buckle was provided by James D. Mullins of Battle Creek, Michigan, and Jim and Dorothy (Mullins) Crenshaw of Murfreesboro, Tennessee. The Mullins family lived in the house from 1918 to 1935, when the home burned. Dorothy was born in the house.

In Culleoka, Tennessee, where Sawney and John Webb first began teaching together in Culleoka Institute, later Culleoka Academy, Betty Gibson and her late husband, Leonard, were my excellent contacts and tour guides. Now retired, Betty is a former postmaster of Culleoka who is also a fine local historian and genealogist.

In Jacksonville, Alabama, once my home away from home, the staffs of the Houston Cole Library at Jacksonville State University, and the Jacksonville Public Library, have been most helpful. The staff at the public library deserves special thanks. Directed by Barbara Rowell, JPL staff members Marissa Brimer (Interlibrary Loan), Brenda Morgan, and Arnetha Turner (History Room) assisted with my use of microfilm loaned from the Louis Round Wilson Special Collections Library, Southern Historical Collection, at the University of North Carolina, Chapel Hill.

I am also thankful to Sarah Bost, Graduate Research Assistant at the Wilson Special Collections Library, for her assistance.

Other professional librarians and archivists have granted my requests and I thank them sincerely for their professionalism. At Duke University in Durham, North Carolina: Amy MacDonald, Assistant University Archivist, Duke University Archives; and David M. Rubenstein Rare Book & Manuscript Library, who was most helpful regarding the former Trinity College Library and the file of Professor Albert M. Webb, John Webb's son. Annie Armour, University Archivist at The University of the South, Sewanee, Tennessee, provided data on John Webb's grandson and namesake, Dr. John Maurice Webb II. Marie (Molly) H. Dohrmann of Special Collections and University Archives at Vanderbilt University Library, Nashville, Tennessee, was very helpful with selections from the Dr. Edwin Mims Papers including personal correspondence between John Webb and his distinguished protégé. At the Tennessee State Library and Archives in Nashville, Frankie King, Librarian, provided necessary bibliographic data. Michael Joseph Klein of the Geography and Map Division at the Library of Congress in Washington, D.C., provided photocopies of the various Sanborn Fire Insurance Maps for Bell Buckle, Tennessee, through 1914. William B. Eigelsbach, Special Collections, Hodges Library, University of Tennessee, Knoxville, was helpful with the 1924 Sanborn Fire Insurance Maps of Bell Buckle, as was Sue Alexander at the James E. Walker Library at Middle Tennessee State University in Murfreesboro. I read newspapers on microfilm at MTSU, as well as at the Nashville (TN) Public Library. Data on the two Latin textbooks published under Confederate imprint by William Bingham of Bingham School came from the Albert and Shirley Small Special Collections Library, University of Virginia Library, in Charlottesville. Kathryn Hopkins and Carolyn Smotherman of the Bedford County Historical Society, Shelbyville, Tennessee, provided a scan of the best image (postcard) of the John Webb home in Bell Buckle, Tennessee. Finally, Carrie Marsh of the Honnold/Mudd Library, Claremont Colleges Library, Claremont University Consortium, Claremont, California, provided the bibliographic data for Laurence McMillin's master's thesis on Sawney Webb.

May Maccallum of the Richmond County Historical Society in Rockingham, North Carolina, enlightened this author about John

Webb's teaching stint at a private academy there before joining his brother, Sawney, in Culleoka, Tennessee. The staff of the Olivia Raney Library in Raleigh, North Carolina, clarified items related to the obituary of Lily Shipp Webb, John's wife. Lynn Richardson, Local History Librarian, North Carolina Collection, at the Durham County Library, Durham, North Carolina, was helpful checking newspapers for Lily Shipp Webb's obituary.

Finally, I found additional information in the following libraries: Argie Cooper Library in Shelbyville, Tennessee (Local History and Genealogy); Birmingham (AL) Public Library, Tutwiler Collection of Southern History and Literature; and in the Heritage Room at the Huntsville-Madison County Public Library in Huntsville, Alabama, my hometown.

On a personal note, my family has been supportive of me throughout this process. Once a family of five, we are now but three, and I thank my sister, Betty Jean (B.J.) Fawley, primary caregiver for our 94-year old father, for allowing me the time and space to complete the research and writing of this book. My nephew, Jeremy Barkley, saved the day by uploading all my files from my imploding old computer to my new laptop. I thank Andrew Havens at Gamecock Computers in Jacksonville, Alabama, for his expert technical assistance. Jeremy Barkley and Kim Bertus also provided vital computer assistance in Huntsville.

My great friend and Civil War historian, Nick Picerno, of Bridgewater College, Bridgewater, Virginia, clarified John Webb's participation in the Confederacy. Old friends Larry Hice of Huntsville, Alabama, and Jim Murray of Birmingham, Alabama, have seen and heard it all before. They have the patience of Job.

Finally, a special thanks must go to Pam Remer Montgomery of Anniston, Alabama, and to Travis Vaughn of Marion, Alabama, for stepping in during the eleventh hour to help me prepare the final manuscript for submission to BrayBree Publishing of Dickson, Tennessee.

I alone am responsible for the content of this work which I humbly present to the reader. I am also the only one to blame.

Terry Barkley
Post Cottage
Monteagle, Tennessee
January 28, 2014

CONTENTS

Foreword *by Margaret Britton Vaughn*	xv
Preface	xvii
Chronology	xxiii
Prologue	xxvii
CHAPTER ONE: Bingham School	3
CHAPTER TWO: Chapel Hill and A Rude Awakening	17
CHAPTER THREE: Learning the Game	21
CHAPTER FOUR: A School of Their Own	33
CHAPTER FIVE: Bell Buckle, Home of Webb School	49
CHAPTER SIX: "God is Often Pleased But Never Satisfied"	53
CHAPTER SEVEN: Success and Concerns	64
CHAPTER EIGHT: Community Near and Far	74
CHAPTARE NINE: Elysian Fields	80
CHAPTER TEN: "Enough to Make the Angels Weep"	83
CHAPTER ELEVEN: "O Love That Wilt Not Let Me Go"	92
CHAPTER TWELVE: A Lasting Legacy	99
CHAPTER THIRTEEN: Sorrowful Angels	104
CHAPTER FOURTEEN: Return to Culleoka and Bell Buckle	112
CHAPTER FIFTEEN: Epilogue	118

Appendix A: Suggestions for Beginning a School Library   123
Appendix B: The Rhodes Scholars of Webb School   131
Appendix C: Did John Webb Serve in the Confederacy?   135
Appendix D: The Sanborn-Perris Fire Insurance Maps
   of Bell Buckle, Tennessee 1894–1924   131
Appendix E: Some Assistant Teachers at Webb School
   (Bell Buckle) 1888–1912   135

Bibliography   137
Index   145
About the Author   161

ILLUSTRATIONS

John M. Webb	Frontispiece
The Sawney Webb home in Culleoka in the early 1870s	22
The Webb School faculty in Bell Buckle circa 1898	34
Student body in front of the Big Room in Bell Buckle in the 1890s	35
John Webb and members of the Senior Class of 1901	36
The 1894 Webb School Tigers football team	40
The Junior Room in Bell Buckle circa 1906	41
The John Webb house in Bell Buckle	54
The 1897–98 Webb School Tennis Club	55
The Sawney Webb house in Bell Buckle	57
Sawney Webb and John Webb in Bell Buckle in the 1890s	65
Advertisement for Webb School placed by John Webb	79
John Andrew Rice and his Caesar class at Webb School	84
Book plate for the John M. Webb Collection	102
Tennessee historical marker for Webb School in Bell Buckle	117
Sanborn-Perris Fire Insurance Map of Bell Buckle in June 1894	133

Unless otherwise credited, all images are courtesy of
The Webb School Archives, Bell Buckle, Tennessee.

FOREWORD

The Brothers Grimm, Jacob and Wilhelm, were folklore scholars who spent years researching hand-me-down stories that became well-known fairytales. Terry Barkley, author of *The Gentle Scholar: The Forgotten Story of John M. Webb and the Webb School of Bell Buckle, Tennessee*, has spent years of impeccable research on the famous Webb School and its founders, William Robert (Sawney) Webb and John Maurice Webb. The Brothers Webb, whom Terry affectionately calls Sawney and John, are more than folklore; they are legends, particularly Sawney. Terry has documented all the tales that have been handed down about these two educators and has unearthed other stories that have lain dormant through the years.

If one just told their story, it would sound like a fairytale, but it is not. Terry Barkley has written the history of Sawney and John Webb, telling their complete story and their founding of Webb School, a classical school for boys with a few girls as day students. Sawney was the rule maker and discipline enforcer, and John was the beloved teacher who was also a superb scholar. As this book points out, students were drawn to John, the gentle scholar. Students feared Sawney because of his strictness but loved John because he opened their minds to learning and culture. Barkley has left nothing out. The book includes every aspect of daily life between the two brothers and their families, including both the pleasant and the unpleasant. Through the years, much has been written about Sawney and very little about John, except in passing. Now Terry offers us a unique lens through which to view John Webb who concentrated on developing the critical thinking of his students.

The internationally recognized Webb School, located in the tiny railroad town of Bell Buckle, Tennessee, has produced Rhodes Scholars, a Pulitzer Prize winner, administrators for United States Presidents, three state governors, college and university presidents, and even contributed to the Honor Code at Princeton University. One of its famous alumni, John Andrew Rice, founded Black Mountain College in North Carolina; incorporating a progressive educational approach, Black Mountain produced noted artists in all walks of life.

Terry mentions many distinguished Americans who have graduated from Webb School, and these alumni have all acknowledged John Webb as a major inspiration for their achievements. Barkley has also featured much of Bell Buckle's history, a small village where town and gown come alive for the reader. Today students from all over the world attend Webb School, which still incorporates the honor code and teaching principles of the Brothers Webb. If the Brothers Grimm were living today, Webb School would be considered the Pied Piper that has led in the academic world and continues to do so today. Terry Barkley has masterfully captured its greatness in *The Gentle Scholar: The Forgotten Story of John M. Webb and the Webb School of Bell Buckle, Tennessee.*

Margaret Britton Vaughn
Poet Laureate of Tennessee

PREFACE

This biography of John M. Webb (1847–1916) is intended to be a companion piece to the late Laurence McMillin's superb work, *The Schoolmaker: Sawney Webb and the Bell Buckle Story* (1971). While I never met Larry McMillin (1923–2005), we did talk once on the telephone about his book, our mutual interests in the Brothers Webb and their classical school, and even of our failed attempts to gain employment at The Webb School in Bell Buckle. An admitted John Webb partisan, it is not my intention to defame Sawney Webb regarding the ugly split between the brothers and their families, only to present the record as I found it. Obviously, it took the combined contributions of Sawney and John Webb as unique "opposites" to produce such a remarkable educational institution as Webb School.

Regarding Webb School and Bell Buckle, please note that it was always just Webb School during the lifetimes of the Brothers Webb. The

Webb School is a later addition, and I use this only in connection with the modern school. Also, it is Hazel Cemetery, not Hazelwood Cemetery, as noted in *The Schoolmaker* and other sources. When I refer to a "Webb Rhodes Scholar," I mean only one of the ten Webb alumni who went on to their respective colleges and universities and who won, at some point, a coveted Rhodes Scholarship for study at Oxford University in England. Finally, when listing class years at Webb School for individuals, this study covers only 1870 to the early 1930s. Thus, '97 would mean 1897, and '07 would be 1907.

My initial introduction to The Webb School in Bell Buckle, Tennessee, came via a one-page tourism article which appeared in the October 1979 issue of *Southern Living* magazine.

Entitled "School Bells at Bell Buckle," I was struck by the mention of Sawney Webb's classroom, the Junior Room, where "ten Rhodes Scholars and the governors of three states" had studied. An accompanying image of several well-dressed students with the tiny Junior Room in the background peaked my interest.

I had been doing some research on the American Rhodes Scholarships to the University of Oxford (Oxford University), and was particularly interested in Rhodes Scholars from state and private military colleges and the service academies. I later branched out to look at Rhodes Scholars from civilian colleges and universities in the South. Obviously, when I learned that "ten Rhodes Scholars" had come from The Webb School, plus the statement in the same article that then-President Woodrow Wilson of Princeton University had considered Webb's graduates among the best students Princeton matriculated, the need to learn more about The Webb School ensued.

At one point, when I was teaching history at Randolph School in Huntsville, Alabama (1975–1978), our concert chorus performed in the auditorium/chapel of the Webb Follin Administration Building at The Webb School in Bell Buckle (I played drum set behind our music director's piano). I remember seeing the Junior Room in its former location in front of Chambliss Dormitory just off Main Street, but I did not have the time to investigate.

Over the past thirty-five years or so, I've made numerous trips to Bell Buckle and the area including several to The Webb School to do research. During the summer of 1991, I volunteered at The Webb School to help rescue the school's battered archives and to try to make some sense of what was there. The archives were then stored in the dark, dingy, and moist basement of the Son Will Building (Admissions). Almost nothing was in any kind of order, and everything was stored in acidic, decaying boxes, some of which had received water damage. Seemingly, all were insect infested.

Nevertheless, what I found was an archivist-historian's dream, a virtual treasure trove of school publications, correspondence including personal letters to and from Sawney and John Webb and others, numerous photographs, and assorted other school memorabilia and ephemera—a goldmine for the serious researcher.

The first step was to remove the archives to a more suitable location in which to work, and that location became a dormitory room in Rand Dormitory, attached to the cafeteria. There I spent the summer months cleaning, sorting, arranging, cataloging, and preserving what I could during my weekends-only trips to Bell Buckle from Huntsville, Alabama, where I worked as the special collections librarian (assistant professor) at Alabama A & M University.

Along the way, I managed to collect over two hundred images and other ephemera and arrange them in a chronological sequence beginning with the Webb Brothers in North Carolina and at Bingham School; Sawney Webb's move to Culleoka, Tennessee, in 1870 (where brother John joined him in 1873); the move to Bell Buckle in 1886; and finally, the "heyday" of Webb School under the Brothers Webb up through the deaths of John Webb in 1916, and Sawney Webb in 1926. Additional material covering the succeeding administration of William Robert Webb Jr., "Son Will," was also accumulated. Finally, I paid special attention to the original Webb School buildings at Bell Buckle, especially the Senior Room and the Junior Room, the classrooms of the Brothers Webb.

Working initially with Margaret (Maggi) Britton Vaughn, Bell Buckle's Poet Laureate of Tennessee, my intention was to publish a photographic history of Webb School as part of the Arcadia Press series published in Charleston, South Carolina, works dealing chiefly with regional and local history which contain mostly images with detailed captions. Entitled "Old Sawney's: A Portrait of Webb School, 1870–1930," I worked up a list of 204 brief captions to accompany the images. All of this material was stored in an acid-free Hollinger box and left in The Webb School Archives dorm room in Rand Dormitory.

A series of events then ensued which thwarted my original plans. Leaving Alabama A & M University that fall, I moved briefly to Bell Buckle and rented a small apartment in an old Victorian home on Maple Street—the same street where both Sawney and John Webb had lived. While continuing to work on the Webb School book idea with the indomitable Maggi Vaughn, I was also looking for employment at The Webb School and in the area. When nothing suitable materialized after several months, I decided to move to Virginia where I joined the staff of the Alexander Mack Library at Bridgewater College in Bridgewater, Virginia. My Webb School book plans were shelved indefinitely, and I served at Bridgewater from 1993 to 2005, dividing my work between archivist in the library and as museum curator of the Reuel B. Pritchett Museum on campus.

Following my part-time summer work at Webb in 1991, Penny Frere, wife of Webb School Headmaster A. Jon Frere, Kimi Abernathy, and others, accomplished significant work in the school's archives in later years.

Following my mother's death in the fall of 2005, I resigned my position at Bridgewater College and returned home to Huntsville, Alabama, to help care for my ailing father. I again visited The Webb School to peruse their archives, only to find that it appeared fairly decimated. At least, what I was shown in a couple of closets was merely a fraction of what had been there originally both in terms of images and in correspondence and printed matter. My chronological collection of images had been dispersed, and I doubted that enough could be reconstructed to revive my original Arcadia Press idea.

Even more time passed and things changed for both The Webb School and for myself. Following a three-year stint as MMI Foundation archivist in the Baer Memorial Library at Marion Military Institute in Marion, Alabama, I completed an additional two years in Elgin, Illinois, as director of the Brethren Historical Library and Archives (BHLA) at the Church of the Brethren General Offices. I retired in the fall of 2012, age 62, to help my sister care for our now 94-year old father, who has Alzheimer's, in his own home in Huntsville, Alabama.

I am happy to report that The Webb School has provided adequate space for their archives in the William Bond Library, the modern hi-tech edifice which replaced the old John Webb Library. The library director, Hannah Byrd Little, and Susan Coop Howell, archivist and librarian's assistant, have done a wonderful job collecting and processing historical materials relating to The Webb School. Various volunteers— including Webb School students and alumni and former faculty and staff members —are assisting in preserving the school's archives and special collections.

CHRONOLOGY

November 27, 1847	John Maurice Webb is born at "Stony Point" in Alamance (later Orange) County, North Carolina, the eleventh child and sixth son of Alexander Smith Webb and Cornelia Adeline (Stanford) Webb.
1849	Alexander Webb dies at age 45, leaving behind his wife and eleven children.
1840s–1850s	John and older brother "Sawney" Webb learn from their first teacher, their sister, Susan Ann "Suny" Webb (1831–1905), in her one-room log school, the "Almeda Schoolhouse."
1862–1864	John studies at the Bingham School at Oaks.

1864–1865	Cadet John M. Webb studies at Bingham School in Mebanesville.
1866–1868	Studies at the University of North Carolina, Chapel Hill, where he is an officer in the Dialectic Society and a junior debater. He receives a diploma from the Dialectic Society.
1869–1870	Begins his teaching career at Bingham School in Mebanesville. He is unhappy and considers resigning.
1870–1873	Serves as principal and teacher at a private academy in Rockingham, Richmond County, North Carolina.
1870	Disgusted with conditions under Reconstruction in North Carolina, Sawney Webb moves to Tennessee. He accepts a teaching position at Culleoka Institute in Culleoka, Tennessee, succeeding Rev. A.G. Dinwiddle, pastor of the Methodist Church, as principal.
January 30, 1873	At Sawney's request, John joins his brother as co-principal of Culleoka Institute.
Spring 1875	Vanderbilt University opens in Nashville, Tennessee. Culleoka Institute alumni are among the first and best students there. John attends the opening exercises.
1875	Receives an honorary AB degree from UNC.
December 7, 1876	Marries Lily Shipp, the daughter of Albert M. and Mary Jane (Gillespie) Shipp of Nashville and Vanderbilt University, in Nashville.
1877	Receives the AM degree from UNC.
1877	John and Lily's first child, Albert Micajah Webb, is born.
1884	New schoolhouse built for the now Culleoka Academy.

Winter 1886	Sawney reportedly "beaten nearly to death" by Culleoka enemies; by February, he is home in North Carolina recuperating. John runs the academy in his absence.
Spring 1886	John and Sawney move to Bell Buckle in Bedford County, Tennessee, to start a classical school of their own, Webb School. Culleoka Academy continues until the building burns around 1900.
August 1886	Webb School opens with three buildings in various stages of completion—the Big Room, the Senior Room (John's classroom and the school library), and the Junior Room (Sawney's classroom).
1886–1887	Homes for the families of John and Sawney Webb are built across from each other on Maple Street in Bell Buckle.
1888	Hazel Alexander Webb, born in 1886 to Lily and John Webb, dies and is buried on a hill in a cemetery named for him outside of Bell Buckle.
1889	Left in charge of the Webb School while Sawney and "Son Will" Webb and two Culleoka alumni go on a summer tour of Europe. John becomes ill and is sent to a sanitarium. Emma Webb and others take charge of the school.
1895	Honorary Doctor of Laws (LLD) degree is conferred upon him by the University of Nashville.
1896–1905	Serves on the executive committee of the Association of Colleges and Prepratory Schools in the Southern States (now Southern Association of Colleges and Schools, SACS).
1897–1898	Serves as vice president of what is now SACS.
August 1897	Attends a gathering of Webb School alumni, students, family, and friends at the Tennessee Centennial and International Exposition in Nashville.

1899–1900	Serves as president of what is now SACS, the first secondary school official elected to that office.
November 27, 1905	On John's 58th birthday, Woodrow Wilson, then president of Princeton University, addresses the students at Webb School, and is entertained in John's home.
1908	William Robert Webb Jr., "Son Will," is made a principal of Webb School alongside Sawney and John Webb.
1911	John and Sawney's disdain for the Carneige Unit academic system comes to a boil.
April 5, 1916	Dies at his home on Maple Street in Bell Buckle at the age of 69. He is buried the next day beside his son Hazel in Hazel Cemetery outside Bell Buckle.
April 7, 1916	Chancellor James H. Kirkland of Vanderbilt University remembers John in a chapel meeting on the Vanderbilt campus. John's family leaves Bell Buckle and Webb School and joins Albert M. Webb and family in Durham, North Carolina.
October 1, 1917	Lily Webb donates the remaining bulk of her husband's private library to Trinity College (later Duke University) in Durham. The collection of nearly 4,000 books includes 2,378 titles, many with multiple volumes. It is a lasting legacy for John Webb.
1927	The Senior Room, John's classroom and the original school library, is torn down to make way for a parking lot.
1927–1928	The John Webb Library is built at Webb School (only the word "Library" is placed on the building).
June 27, 1929	Wife Lily Webb dies in Durham, North Carolina, at the age of 80. Her body is brought back to Bell Buckle to rest beside her husband and son, each in unmarked graves.

PROLOGUE

THE WISDOM BUMP

"Old Johnny" was on the move again, taking his daily constitutional through the streets of Bell Buckle and along the railroad tracks. The gentle scholar, head down, mumbling to himself in several languages, was always a welcome sight to students and "townies" alike in Bell Buckle. Universally loved and respected by all who knew or even met him, one realized that, regardless of their station in life, the old teacher accepted them for who they were and on their own terms. His students loved him for his inspiration and life-long friendship, and university administrators and professors deferred to him for his comprehensive life-long learning.

John Maurice Webb had a wisdom bump on his high forehead. Students joked that he knew so much that he had to have an extra compartment to store the overflow of knowledge. It was the first thing many people noticed about him. While the truth remained that the wisdom bump was the unhappy result of contact with a cow as a youth, it nevertheless helped to solidify John Webb's reputation as a scholar of the first order and as a master teacher and co-principal of Webb School. A beloved and respected educator for some forty-seven years—forty-three years with his brother, Sawney—until John's death in 1916, the Brothers Webb, both bearded and similar-looking physically, combined their unique talents as "opposites" to forge one of the finest college preparatory schools in the nation.

The Gentle Scholar

CHAPTER ONE

BINGHAM SCHOOL

He lies buried in an unmarked grave. His house has burned down and another now occupies the site. His classroom at Webb School in Bell Buckle, Tennessee, the Senior Room, was torn down to make way for a parking lot. A modern, high-tech library named for someone else has replaced the school library that once bore his name. Even the village bank where he once served as president no longer stands. While his older brother, William Robert "Sawney" Webb—the recognized founder of Webb School—is legendary, few today remember the younger brother and his unique contributions not only to Webb School and Bell Buckle, but to Vanderbilt University and the improvement of educational standards throughout Tennessee and the South from the post-Reconstruction period to the early 20th century.

John Maurice Webb was known as "the gentle scholar." He was a master teacher who served as co-principal of the famed Webb School for forty-three years. Founded in Culleoka, Tennessee, by "Sawney" Webb of Oaks, North Carolina, in 1870, John joined his older brother three years later in a joint family venture that eventually produced one of the more remarkable educational institutions not only in Tennessee and the South, but nationwide. The Webb School moved to Bell Buckle in 1886 and recently celebrated its 144th anniversary as one of the prominent private boarding and day schools in the country.

Vermont Royster, Webb School Class of 1931 and later Pulitzer Prize-winning editor of *The Wall Street Journal*, wrote that in the first fifty years of Webb School, the brothers Webb taught more students who went on to receive Rhodes Scholarships to the University of Oxford in England than any other secondary educational institution in America to that time. Nine alumni became future Rhodes Scholars during the lifetime and service of Sawney Webb, who died in 1926; eight of those nine also studied with John Webb, who passed in 1916. A tenth future Rhodes Scholar was graduated later. In addition, Webb alumni included a U.S. Senator from Tennessee, the governors of three states, at least four future college and university presidents attended Webb School during the period, and a vast array of Webb Old Boys and Girls achieved distinction and prominence in their chosen careers and professions.

Reminiscing on a time when he was president of Princeton University, Woodrow Wilson, twenty-eighth President of the United States, remarked, "The best students we get come from a small school in Tennessee known to its pupils as 'Old Sawney's.'"[1] Wilson visited the Webb brothers at their school in Bell Buckle in 1905 and delivered an address before the student body.[2] When Wilson became president, at least two Webb School graduates served in his administration. In fact, the honor code at Princeton University, the famed "Princeton System," was initi-

---

1. Randolph Elliott, "Old Sawney's." *The Atlantic Monthly* (August 1920), 231. Edd Winfield Parks, "Sawney Webb: Tennessee's Schoolmaster." *Segments of Southern Thought* (Athens, GA: The University of Georgia Press, 1938), 268. "School Bells at Bell Buckle," *Southern Living* (October 1979), 44.

2. Woodrow Wilson, President's Room, Princeton University, Princeton, New Jersey, to Mr. W. R. Webb, Bell Buckle, Tennessee, November 22, 1905, The Webb School Archives. Glenn N. Holliman, "The Webb School Junior Room, The Symbol of a School," *Tennessee Historical Quarterly*, Vol. 36, No. 3 (Fall 1977), 299.

ated by a Webb School graduate attending Princeton who emulated the honor code at Webb, a fact acknowledged by Princeton University.[3]

The gentle scholar was a shy, retiring soul, ever the classic "bookworm" who took little notice of the affairs of his day. A storehouse of knowledge, a walking personification of the absent-minded professor, John Webb's mantle was character. He stressed the Biblical admonition to gain understanding while gaining knowledge, and he believed that understanding would elicit patience and humility. His home—domain of his loving wife and adoring children, and filled to the brim with his extensive private library—served as his sanctuary; but his classroom at Webb School, the Senior Room, which doubled as the original school library in Bell Buckle, provided the forum whereby John Webb daily challenged the minds of Webb School's best students. The late Laurence McMillin, Sawney Webb's biographer, referred to the Senior Room—a "peak-roofed box of a building"—as "a modest residence of high civilization…an entrance to the Elysian Fields." Thus in time, the Senior Room became a holy place to those students fortunate enough to come under Old Johnny's (later, Old Jack's) spell.[4]

Rhodes Scholar John Andrew Rice, a Webb Old Boy who returned from Oxford University to teach in Bell Buckle for two years, readily identified John Webb as his ideal teacher-philosopher. The controversial Rice, founder and first rector of the experimental Black Mountain College in North Carolina, considered John Webb the quintessential master teacher.[5]

The same was true for another Webb Rhodes Scholar, William Yandell Elliott, a Vanderbilt graduate counted among that university's famed Fugitives and Agrarians groups. Dr. Elliott later served as a distinguished professor of history and government at Harvard University and American University, and as a political advisor to six U.S. presidents. Among

---

3. H. G. Murray, Secretary, The Graduate Council of Princeton University, Princeton, New Jersey, to Mr. W. R. Webb Jr., Bell Buckle, Tennessee, July 13, 1916, The Webb School Archives.

4. Laurence McMillin, *The Schoolmaker: Sawney Webb and the Bell Buckle Story* (Chapel Hill, NC: The University of North Carolina Press, 1971), 130.

5. Mary Emma Harris, *The Arts of Black Mountain College* (Cambridge, MA: MIT Press, 1987), 8, Bibliography: 303–304. See also Martin Duberman, *Black Mountain: An Exploration in Community* (New York: E.P. Dutton & Co., Inc., 1972), 22.

Elliott's outstanding students at Harvard, he mentored future U.S. Secretary of State Henry Kissinger.[6]

But among John Webb's numerous friends and admirers, Webb Old Boy Dr. Edwin Mims, long-time head of the dynamic English Department at Vanderbilt University and a man at the forefront of the development of a Southern literary tradition, put it best: the "gentle scholar" would always be remembered as "John, the Beloved."[7]

John Maurice Webb was born at home at Stony Point, near Oaks, in Alamance (later Orange) County, North Carolina, on November 27, 1847. The son of Alexander Smith Webb (1804–1849) and Cornelia Adeline Stanford Webb (1811–1891), he was the eleventh of twelve children born (one died) and the sixth of seven sons. His family was of Scots-Irish descent. Alexander S. Webb died at age forty-five several months before his last child, Samuel Henry, was born. John was barely nineteen months old at the time. With the father dead, the mother and second oldest daughter, Cornelia and Susan, respectively, served as the all-important teachers for the children.[8]

In 1845, the Alexander Webb family left their farm, Harmony Hill, in the highlands of Person County, North Carolina—in the shadow of Old Virginia—and headed further south. They moved to a worn-out farm and inadequate farmhouse called "Stony Point" near Oaks, North Carolina. The Webbs brought their "servants" with them, as they never called their human property "slaves." The Webb family specifically moved to Oaks to be near the noted select school of the Bingham family.[9]

---

6. *Address of William Yandell Elliott To The Class of 1960*, Webb School, Bell Buckle, Tennessee, 90th Commencement, June 8, 1960, The Webb School Archives. "Who are The Rhodes Scholars of Webb School?" The Webb School, *Alumni Bulletin* (Spring 1977), 6.

7. Edwin Mims, "John Maurice Webb (1847–1916)," An address delivered at Webb School commencement, June 5, 1946, in connection with the 75th anniversary of the founding of Webb School (Nashville, TN: [s.n.], 1946), 25.

8. John Webb's birthdate is sometimes given as November 29, as it is in Laurence McMillin's *The Schoolmaker*. "Webb, John Maurice," *Who's Who in America*, Vol. 9, 1916–1917 (Chicago, IL: A.N. Marquis & Co., 1916), 2603, is among a number of sources which gives the correct birth date of November 27. McMillin, 14. Emma Webb McLean, *Sawney Webb: Maker of Men*. Privately published (Laverne, CA: Preston Printing, 1969), 8–9.

9. McMillin, 12–13.

In addition to John's mother, Cornelia, two of his siblings figured prominently in his life—Susan Ann "Suny" Webb (1831–1905), John's older sister; and William Robert "Sawney" Webb (1842–1926), his older brother and eventual life-long partner in teaching. Susan, a natural-born teacher, served as the first teacher for both Sawney and John, as well as the other children at Stony Point, teaching in her own one-room log school called the "Almeda Schoolhouse."[10]

Sawney Webb had been born in the Webb farmhouse at Harmony Hill near Mount Tirzah in Person County, North Carolina, on November 11, 1842. Sawney was a family nickname. He was just six-and-half when his father died in 1849.

Growing up in a large farm family, John stayed active with his daily chores and helping out where needed. He had a wisdom bump on his high forehead, the result of being gored by a cow. While certainly noticeable, it was not unsightly. As he grew, John began developing a passion for books on any subject and he was constantly reading and learning whenever an opportunity presented itself.

Sawney was nearly fourteen when he started at the Bingham's school nearby in 1856.[11] Similarly, following in his brother's footsteps, John attended the Bingham School at Oaks, Orange County, from 1862 to 1864, and in Mebanesville (Mebane Station, later Mebane), Alamance County, in 1865, when the school was moved there to be near the railroad. Sawney would teach at Bingham School briefly in 1865, and John would return after studying at the University of North Carolina, Chapel Hill, to begin his teaching career at Bingham School in Mebanesville from 1869 to 1870.

The Bingham family of great teachers reigned over North Carolina for more than 135 years and spanning three centuries. Their schools were chiefly classical schools centered primarily on Latin, Greek, and mathematics. At Oaks, the Bingham School was considered not only the best

---

10. McMillin, 15–16. Buried in the cemetery of the Bethlehem Presbyterian Church (circa 1822) at Oaks are Alexander Smith and Cornelia Adeline Webb, Susan "Suny" Webb, and Samuel Henry Webb, among other family members.

11. McMillin, 20. Matthew Hodgson, "Webb, William Robert (Sawney)," *Dictionary of North Carolina Biography*, Vol. 6 (Chapel Hill, NC: The University of North Carolina Press), 151, states that Sawney Webb attended Hillsborough Academy under William James Bingham, beginning at the age of twelve. This appears plausible as even the Bingham offspring were finishing at Bingham School by age fourteen.

preparatory school in the Tar Heel state, but one of the finest in the entire South. The Binghams always claimed that Bingham School dated from 1793, when Reverend William Bingham (1754–1826) taught school in Wilmington, North Carolina. He later moved to the Piedmont region of the state where he opened Chatham Academy, taught ancient languages for four years at the University of North Carolina, and later taught at Pittsborough Academy and Hillsborough Academy before opening his own school in the country at Mount Repose by 1815. Bingham served as principal of private academies for some thirty-three years until his death. His son, William James Bingham (1802–1866), called the "Napoleon of schoolmasters," assumed his father's position at Mount Repose before becoming principal at Hillsborough Academy. Boasting over a hundred students and enjoying a nation-wide reputation, the tuition of $150 per year at Hillsborough Academy was possibly the highest in the nation for a preparatory school. In 1844, like his father, William James established his own academy on his farm in rural Oaks, some eleven miles west of Chapel Hill. Bingham reduced the student body to thirty, gradually raising it to about sixty male scholars. It was the Webb family's move from Person County to Oaks which allowed Sawney, John, and other Webb boys to get the very best education available at that time.[12]

The Bingham School's alumni distinguished themselves as professional men in all walks of life including educators such as James Horner of Horner (Classical) School in Oxford, North Carolina, and Sawney and John Webb in Culleoka and Bell Buckle (Webb School), Tennessee. They were in the company of numerous preachers, missionaries, theologians, statesmen, politicians, soldiers, businessmen, and literati who sprang from North Carolina's finest preparatory school, including at least three North Carolina governors. Distinguished journalist Walter Hines Page became U.S. ambassador to Great Britain during World War I, as

---

12. Robert I. Curtis, "The Bingham School and Classical Education in North Carolina, 1793–1873," *The North Carolina Historical Review*, Vol. LXXIII, No. 3 (July 1996), 338–339. Bennett L. Steelman, "Bingham, William (1754–1826)," and "Bingham, William James (1802–1866)," *Dictionary of North Carolina Biography*, Vol. 1, 159–160, 161. Although the school building at Oaks is gone, the Bingham farmhouse survives and is today a delightful bed & breakfast known as "The Inn at Bingham School." Guests can even stay in the Headmaster's Room. The house is listed on the National Register for Historic Places and was an award-winning restoration of the National Trust Project in 1984.

would Robert Worth Bingham, who served as U.S. ambassador to Great Britain, Court of St. James, in the 1930s.[13]

At Oaks, beginning in 1844, William James Bingham operated a successful farm and built his own school some 200 yards from his farmhouse. He first advertised his private school as a "Select Classical and Mathematical School," and later as "W. J. Bingham's Select School," emphasizing that he would accept only good boys generally between the ages of ten and fourteen. The school was first advertised as the Bingham School in 1861, but did not officially become such until 1864. The school attracted boys from some of the South's leading families, families that could pay the $80 annual tuition, then among the most expensive in the country.[14]

First constructed of logs, then of brick, giving it a look of permanence and belying the "portability" scheme set by the Binghams and followed by the Brothers Webb, the schoolhouse contained "three classrooms and was fronted by a long, brick-columned piazza that ran the full length of the building." The scholars boarded in private homes in the area including the hospitable Webb home at Stony Point and in the Bingham farmhouse on site. The academic year was divided into two five-month sessions beginning in July and again in January and commencing at the end of May, and stressed Latin, Greek, mathematics, and English, generally. In time, the Bingham School acquired a national reputation for its educational excellence, and applications to the school always exceeded its vacancies.[15]

On December 9, 1864, late in the Civil War, the North Carolina General Assembly passed "An Act to Incorporate Bingham School," which effectively transformed Bingham into both a military and classical school. The school's superintendent and its instructors received commissions in the state militia, and the students, now cadets undergoing military training and discipline, were exempt from military service until the age of eighteen. However, the school was subject to mobilization as a separate military unit in the event of local emergency, as was the case during Stoneman's Raid in 1865. Cadet John M. Webb served guard duty at Oaks carrying a rusty musket.[16] By the end of December 1864,

13. Curtis, 329–330.
14. Curtis, 349.
15. Curtis, 346, 350.
16. Curtis, 352. McMillin, 38.

Colonel William Bingham, son of William James, moved the school from Oaks to Mebanesville, in eastern Alamance County, to be near the North Carolina Railroad with its transport and potential supplies. The lack of suitable student boarding homes in the Oaks area late in the war was a contributing factor in relocating the school to Mebanesville.[17]

The Bingham School managed to remain open throughout the Civil War save for a brief period during Major General George Stoneman's Union cavalry raid in North Carolina during March and April 1865, when the student body/cadet corps was called to active duty. John Webb was a student cadet at the time but probably only served guard duty along the railway.

Brother Sawney was briefly a faculty member at Bingham School in Mebanesville about the time of Stoneman's raid. An official state roster of five militia officers for "Bingham School," including Colonel William Bingham as superintendent, lists Captain William R. Webb as a "professor" as of March 8, 1865.[18]

William Bingham was not only a recognized educator, but a fine scholar. During the Civil War he wrote two classical textbooks, both published under Confederate imprint, *A Grammar of the Latin Language* (1863), and an edited translation of Caesar's *Commentaries on the Gallic Wars* (1864). These texts were used by the Brothers Webb both in Culleoka and in Bell Buckle. With later editions, both texts were utilized in numerous schools around the United States for decades, both textbooks remaining in print for over twenty-five years. Bingham produced *A Grammar of the English Language* in 1867, and a series of Latin readers. At the time of his death on February 18, 1873, thirty-seven year-old William Bingham was preparing a textbook on Latin prose composition. A Presbyterian elder, noted speaker and orator, accomplished pianist and organist, and occasional poet, William Bingham was buried in the Mebane City Cemetery near his father, William James Bingham, and other family members.[19]

Although the Bingham family chose 1793 as the founding of Bingham School, the school was officially chartered by the State of North

---

17. Curtis, 352–353, note 140.

18. Stephen E. Bradley, *North Carolina Confederate Militia Officers Roster*, ed. by Stephen E. Bradley Jr. (Wilmington, NC: Broadfoot Publishing Company, 1992), 316.

19. Steelman, *Dictionary of North Carolina Biography*, Vol. 1, 160. Curtis, 353–354, 359.

Carolina while at Oaks in 1864. Binghams had taught in the North Carolina towns of Wilmington, Pittsboro, Mt. Repose, and Hillsborough, before moving to Oaks in 1844. Additional moves in North Carolina as Bingham School and Bingham Military School included to Mebanesville (Mebane) in December, 1864, and the final move to Asheville in 1891. Bingham Military School closed its doors in 1928. The Bingham family business emphasized that bricks and mortar do not constitute a school, and that buildings could also be "portable," an educational concept not lost on the Brothers Webb.[20]

In comparison to the Binghams, Sawney Webb always dated the founding of Webb School to 1870, when he moved from North Carolina to Culleoka, Tennessee. However, the school there was first Culleoka Institute and then Culleoka Academy during the sixteen years Sawney, with John, who joined him in 1873, taught in Culleoka. Only with the move to Bell Buckle in 1886, did Webb School officially come into existence. Obviously, the John Webb family would later view the move to Bell Buckle as a new beginning for the brothers including the unwritten but implied contract that both brothers shared equally in the school and that both would continue to lead the school as co-principals.

Sawney Webb entered the University of North Carolina at age seventeen, and with the outbreak of the Civil War, postponed his studies to join Company H (Alamance County), Fifteenth North Carolina Infantry Regiment as first sergeant. Sawney was wounded in action (right arm) at Malvern Hill in Virginia on July 1, 1862. While recuperating from his wounds, he taught briefly at the Horner (Classical) School in

---

20. Paul Barringer, a renowned physician and educator, attended Bingham School in Mebanesville beginning in August, 1871, after John Webb's painful one-year teaching assignment. Barringer recorded his memories of the Bingham brothers, William and Robert, along with an excellent description of the school and its inner workings in Mebanesville in *The Natural Bent* (1949). His father, Confederate General Rufus Clay Barringer, was captured on April 3, 1865, at Namozine Church in Virginia. While imprisoned at City Point prison, Barringer became the first Confederate general to meet Abraham Lincoln. Paul Barringer's paternal grandfather, General Paul Barringer, served in the U.S. Army during the War of 1812, and his maternal grandfather, the Reverend Robert Hall Morrison, was the first president of Davidson College in North Carolina. His mother's sisters were married to Confederate Generals Thomas J. "Stonewall" Jackson and Daniel H. Hill. See Paul Brandon Barringer, *The Natural Bent: The Memoirs of Dr. Paul B. Barringer* (Chapel Hill, NC: The University of North Carolina Press, 1949), 119–121, 151–162. Marcus B. Simpson Jr., "Barringer, Paul Brandon (1857–1941)," and Marvin Krieger, "Barringer, Rufus Clay (1821–1895)," *Dictionary of North Carolina Biography*, Vol. 1, 102. McMillin, 41.

Oxford, North Carolina, in 1863, and continued his studies in Chapel Hill. Later, Sawney became a cavalryman in Company K, Second North Carolina Cavalry, and rode with Wade Hampton and J.E.B. Stuart in Virginia. In March 1865, he was listed as being on the faculty of Bingham School in Mebanesville, where brother John was a student cadet. However, on April 5, 1865, Sawney was captured at Amelia Court House, Virginia, and imprisoned on Hart's Island in New York Harbor. Sawney's escape from prison, his lone sojourn into New York City in his Confederate uniform, and his subsequent decision to escape back into prison, are legendary.[21]

Sawney taught again at Horner School (later, Horner Military School) in Oxford, North Carolina, from 1865 to 1869. There he was addressed as "Captain" Webb, as he had been as a "professor" at Bingham School in early 1865. Sawney was awarded the AB degree from UNC in 1867, and the AM degree the following year.

Addressed to "My Dearest Friend," R.B. Willcox, a Confederate soldier imprisoned at Elmira, New York, and later sent to Petersburg, Virginia, to be exchanged and returned home, sent two letters to John Webb at Oaks, Orange County, that survive in the Webb Family Papers at Chapel Hill. They are dated September 3, 1864, from Elmira and November 19, 1864, from Petersburg. John's brother, James H., also a prisoner, was sending letters to the family at Oaks from Fort Delaware in Delaware, and from Camp Chase in Ohio. Sawney would later write from prison on Hart's Island in New York Harbor.[22]

John Webb's family at Stony Point normally rented to student boarders from the Bingham School at Oaks. John, himself an academic star from the very beginning, scored first in every subject except arithmetic, where the "passable" he received shamed the sensitive young scholar.[23]

Dr. Edwin Mims, John Webb's protégé, academic "son," friend, and confidant, later wrote of John's record at Bingham School:

---

21. McMillin, 31–44. Hodgson, "Webb, William Robert (Sawney)," *Dictionary of North Carolina Biography*, Vol. 6, 151. Ridley Wills II, "Webb, William R. "Sawney" (1842–1926)," *The Tennessee Encyclopedia of History & Culture*, Tennessee Historical Society (Nashville, TN: Rutledge Hill Press, 1998), 1044.

22. Webb Family Papers (Webb-Moore Papers), Southern Historical Collection, University of North Carolina, Chapel Hill, Microfilm (MF), Reel 1.

23. McMillin, 39.

I have seen the record of his school achievement from 1862 to 1865. During his last year he made an average of forty-nine and thirteen-seventeenths out of a possible perfect grade of fifty. Another term he made an average of forty-nine and a half. The thoroughness with which the teaching was done is indicated in the division of Greek and Latin into "reading, analysis, composition." In mathematics he was "perfect." His conduct was always "exemplary."[24]

---

24. Mims, 32.

William Bingham, Robert Bingham, and Robert Worth Bingham

William Bingham (1835–1873), William James's eldest son, finished at his father's school at Oaks in 1849 at the age of fourteen. Considered too young to enter the University of North Carolina, he worked on the family farm until 1853, when he finally entered UNC in Chapel Hill, graduating in 1856 with first honors. William took a master's degree there in 1859, while continuing to teach in his father's school.

Robert (1838–1927), youngest son of William James, studied at his father's school from 1849–1853. He also graduated from the University of North Carolina with first honors, and began teaching at Oaks in 1857. William James taught the beginning classes—like Sawney Webb would later in his own school—while his sons taught the more advanced scholars.

Both William and Robert were admitted as junior partners in the firm of W.J. Bingham and Sons in 1857.

With the outbreak of the Civil War, William, always in precarious health, remained with his aging and ailing father to run the school, assuming everyday management by 1864. He was, however, appointed colonel of the Forty-seventh Regiment of North Carolina Militia, and later placed in charge of hunting down Confederate deserters in the region.

Robert, who took an MA degree at Chapel Hill in 1860, went to war in 1862 as captain of Company G, Forty-fourth North Carolina Infantry. He was captured in the action at South Anna Bridge in Virginia on June 26, 1863. Imprisoned at Johnson's Island and Fort Delaware until April 1864, he was exchanged at Point Lookout, Maryland. Robert Bingham then rejoined his regiment and fought until it surrendered with Lee's Army of Northern Virginia on Palm Sunday, April 9, 1865, at Appomattox Court House in Virginia. He was paroled a captain, but enjoyed the honorific rank of "major" at Bingham School in Mebanesville, where he returned to teach. Robert was later commissioned a colonel in the North Carolina National Guard. On his father's death in 1866, Robert became co-principal with his brother, William.

When William died in 1873, Robert became headmaster and, after buying out another investor in 1879, became sole head of Bingham School. Under Robert's leadership, Bingham School enhanced its national reputation and gained acceptance from the U.S. Army as an educational and military training center. Commissioned officers were assigned there as professors of military science and tactics after 1882. The Bingham School moved once again, its final move, to "Bingham Heights" in Asheville, North Carolina, in 1891. The physical plant, located above the French Broad River, would sport the first gymnasium and swimming pool ever built for a secondary school in the South.

Though headmaster of a renowned private military preparatory school, Robert Bingham was a strong advocate for public education including compulsory education, teacher education, and women's educational training in North Carolina. Illness forced him to retire in 1920, and the future of Bingham Military School was entrusted to a board of trustees which had been created in 1904. However, after Colonel Bingham died in Asheville on May 8, 1927, the school was closed in the autumn of 1928, supposedly to carry out major new construction and renovation costing a quarter of a million dollars. Bingham Military School never reopened and there was no public explanation as to why. The reasons for its closure remain speculative to this day. Robert Bingham, Presbyterian elder, life member of the National Education Association (NEA), active Mason, and prolific writer and speaker on Southern affairs, was buried in Riverside Cemetery in Asheville. In all, he led Bingham School for some fifty-four years, the final thirty-six years in Asheville. Awarded an honorary doctorate from the University of North Carolina in 1891, Bingham Hall was named in his honor on the University campus in 1929. In 1939, a memorial tablet in his name was installed in Memorial Hall on campus.[1]

Robert Bingham's son, Robert Worth, was born in Mebane in 1871, finished at Bingham School in 1888, and graduated Phi Beta Kappa from the University of North Carolina in 1891. He pursued graduate work at the University of Virginia, taught at Bingham School for two years, then returned to the University of North Carolina to study law, finally receiving his law degree from the University of Louisville in Kentucky in 1897. Publisher of the *Louisville Courier Journal* and the *Louisville Times*, he served as U.S. ambassador to Great Britain, Court of St. James, from 1933–1937.

1. Curtis, 328–329, 374–375. Bennett L. Steelman, "Bingham, William (1835–1873)," and "Bingham, Robert (1838–1927)," *Dictionary of North Carolina Biography*, Vol. 1, 157–158, 160–161.

In 1916, Bingham married his second wife, Mary Lily (Kenan) Flagler, widow of Henry M. Flagler, a cofounder of Standard Oil Company with John D. Rockefeller, and a prime developer of Florida's east coast. When Mrs. Bingham died suddenly at her home in Louisville in 1917, she left an estate of almost $100 million. After her will was bitterly contested, Robert Bingham received $5 million and endowed the Kenan professorships at the University of North Carolina. He died on December 18, 1937, and was buried in Cave Hill Cemetery in Louisville. Robert Worth Bingham received honorary doctorates from the University of Louisville and from the Universities of London, Cambridge, and Oxford in Great Britain.[2]

2. Steelman, "Bingham, Robert Worth (1871–1937)," *Dictionary of North Carolina Biography*, Vol. 1, 158–159. See David Leon Chandler, with Mary Voelz Chandler, *The Binghams of Louisville: The Dark History Behind One of America's Great Fortunes* (New York: Crown Publishers, Inc., 1987).

CHAPTER TWO

CHAPEL HILL
AND A RUDE AWAKENING

Although John Webb wanted desperately to attend Thomas Jefferson's "academical village" at the University of Virginia in Charlottesville, the added expense was prohibitive to the family's fortunes. This was particularly true as Sawney Webb was also trying to send youngest brother Sam to Washington College in Lexington, Virginia, where Robert E. Lee had accepted the presidency after the war. Thus John followed Sawney to the University of North Carolina at Chapel Hill, some eleven miles east from Oaks, where he immediately obtained sophomore status. John attended the University for two and a half years from 1866 to 1868.[1]

---

1. McMillin, 54. Samuel Henry Webb graduated in the Class of 1870 at Washington College, the year General Robert E. Lee died at his home on campus, and the year Sawney Webb moved to Culleoka, Tennessee. Sam became a lawyer at home in Oaks; he is buried in the Bethlehem Presbyterian Church cemetery along with his sister, Susan ("Suny"), and their parents, among

The University of North Carolina was moribund when John arrived on campus, an institution that had loomed large in the South before the war. A year after Appomattox, Chapel Hill was nearly deserted in 1866, and only a few professors and students remained. Nevertheless, John found one or two professors who inspired his intellectual curiosity, and the University library became the gateway to the world for the young scholar's budding interests.

John joined the Dialectic Society at UNC and held the offices of recorder, secretary, librarian, vice-president, and archives keeper. He was elected one of two junior debaters in February 1868, and on June 4, 1868, he asked for and received a diploma from the Dialectic Society. Because the University closed from 1871–1875 during Reconstruction following the Civil War, John was not granted an honorary AB degree until 1875. He received the AM degree from UNC in 1877.[2]

Sawney did all he could to ensure John's success at Chapel Hill, even paying for additional reference books and supplies that John wanted and felt he needed. "My dear John," Sawney wrote. "Yes, go ahead! Get the best reference books—I want you to be a scholar. The fulfillment of your wishes means as much to me as the fulfillment of my own."[3]

John's first teaching assignment was an unhappy one, a rude awakening not unlike that for countless other beginning or first-year teachers. He quickly learned that being a student in the classroom and actually teaching in one while maintaining classroom discipline were two very different experiences. John had been looking like a "hot house plant" for want of exercise, according to his sister Susan. Then he was ill in the fall of 1868. By early 1869, however, John was teaching at Bingham School in Mebanesville, his alma mater, a trying ordeal for the mild and meek

---

other family members. See *Washington & Lee University Alumni Directory, 1749-1985*, "Class of 1870" (White Plains, NY: Bernard C. Harris Publishing Company, Inc., 1986), 132. According to Emma Webb McLean, a letter from Robert E. Lee regarding Sam Webb's record at Washington College (now Washington & Lee University) was among the treasures stored in the attic of the old home place in Oaks, North Carolina. See McLean, 38.

2. Eva Burbank Murphy, "Webb, John Maurice," *Dictionary of North Carolina Biography*, Vol. 6, 1996, 148–149. Hodgson, "Webb, William Robert (Sawney)," *Dictionary of North Carolina Biography*, Vol. 6, 151.

3. McLean, 38.

young educator who was no match for those larger, aggressive boys who could and did intimidate their teacher at every opportunity.[4]

Colonel William Bingham wrote to Sawney at the end of March regarding John:

> He does his work faithfully and efficiently & accomplishes all I expect of him, but his position is an unpleasant one, and he has become depressed & discouraged beyond measure, so as to talk seriously of quitting his post. He imagines that he does not command the respect of the boys and feels with a keenness which none but a very sensitive nature knows, the little differences in demeanor which boys make between myself & him.

Sawney hurriedly wrote to John:

> Don't become discouraged in spirit. If you find yourself brooding over difficulties, bury y'r thoughts in some mathematical problem or some book or pay a visit—anything to get away from y'r thoughts. We are just alike, haven't enough self-confidence and hence under[r]ate ourselves. We must struggle against it with all our might. With prayer to God, we may be able to overcome every obstacle that is in our path.

The Brothers Webb had already decided to join forces someday as teaching partners, hopefully in a school of their very own. They had talked in this vein as early as Sawney's Horner School days in Oxford, North Carolina, but that opportunity never materialized. Both brothers needed to be where they could thrive as teachers, and both needed to be together, combining their own unique talents as "opposites." Yielding to John as the intellectual "star" in this partnership, Sawney wrote to John: "In consequence of my failure to finished my course…I will have to do drudgery all my days and stick to the grammar & dictionary. You will have to do the polishing for the firm of Webb & Company."[5]

Leaving the faculty of Bingham School in 1870, John became principal and teacher of a private academy in Rockingham, Richmond County,

4. McMillin, 54.
5. McMillin, 54.

North Carolina, from 1870 to 1873. According to the 1870 census, he stayed with a Covington family in Wolf Pit, Richmond County.[6]

John Webb appears to have been successful in the private academy in Rockingham; this success provided a much needed boost to his fragile confidence that he could indeed become the teacher of his dreams.

Meanwhile, big brother and eventual teaching partner Sawney was enjoying success of his own teaching in a moldy church basement in tiny Culleoka, Tennessee.

---

6. According to data supplied this author by May Maccallum of the Richmond County Historical Society in Rockingham, North Carolina, June 6, 2013, the academy in question was probably the Rockingham Sabbath School. The Covington family name appears on the student roster. One of the school's record books survives in the Leak-Wall Papers of the Southern Historical Collection, SHC # 1468, Vol. S-1, at the University of North Carolina, Chapel Hill. The Covington family was probably the Benjamin Harrison Covington family in the 1870 census. Mr. Covington was either deceased or otherwise out of the picture as his wife, Mary Ann Harlee, appeared to be head of household. A Mary Dockery, perhaps another teacher, was also living in the house.

CHAPTER THREE

LEARNING THE GAME

Disgusted with conditions in North Carolina during Reconstruction, Sawney Webb decided to go west to seek his fame and fortune as a school teacher. He traveled to Tennessee, where he believed Reconstruction conditions were over, and rode the rails up and down stopping in villages and towns seeking a job teaching. Following a number of disappointments, providence led him to stop off at Pleasant Grove Station just above the village of Culleoka in Maury County, Tennessee. There he finally secured a teaching position.

Culleoka Institute was founded in 1867 in the basement of the new Methodist Church with Reverend A.G. Dinwiddie serving as both pastor of the church and principal of the school. Sawney Webb became the principal in 1870, joined by brother John as co-principal in 1873. The school was incorporated in March 1884 in its new "commodious building" west of the church as Culleoka Academy, Sawney Webb being one

The Sawney Webb home in Culleoka in the early 1870s. Sawney sits in a rocking chair while his wife Emma stands behind him. The slender hatted man standing on the balcony may be John Webb. Student boarders are among this group. The African American women are employees of the Webb family.

of seven incorporators listed. For some sixteen years, from Sawney's arrival in Culleoka in 1870, and until their move to Bell Buckle in 1886, the Brothers Webb created one of the finest preparatory schools in Tennessee, if not the South. At its height, some 130 students boarded in and around Culleoka.[1]

Culleoka, Tennessee, platted in 1857 but unincorporated, is some ten miles from Columbia, the county seat of Maury County. Pleasant Grove Station, a half mile north of the village, once served the Nashville and Decatur Railroad. The town had a bank and other businesses, most of which burned in various fires, but there were also as many as thirty-six small distilleries in that part of the county in its early days. The Webbs were strict prohibitionists. *The Century Review* of Maury County stated:

---

1. Organized in the late 1850s, the Methodist Church in Culleoka was supposedly built circa 1866–1867. The basement school reportedly started there in 1867. Several sources state that the church was not built until 1868.

"…if it were not for the baneful influence of saloons, the Christian people would be happy."[2]

When school opened in Culleoka in January 1873 with 103 students, too many for just one teacher, Sawney wrote to John in Rockingham, North Carolina, to come quickly. John, while enjoying success as the principal and teacher of a private academy, found his work neither rewarding nor prosperous financially. He replied to Sawney on January 13th that he was "coming after the 'bbl. [barrel] of money.'" Sawney responded by announcing his brother's arrival in the *Herald* on January 24th:

> John M. Webb has become associate Principal…first honor man at the University of N. C. under the OLD FACULTY. …The principals hope by their joint efforts to make the school in the future more worthy of the liberal patronage with which it has been heretofore favored. Room for a few more good boys…[3]

John Webb arrived in Culleoka on January 30, 1873, sporting a new beaver hat. Sawney often said that John was "the greatest scholar I have ever seen," and the two brothers were elated to be finally joining forces as educators. In the circulars for Culleoka Institute and later Culleoka Academy, John was listed with Sawney as co-principal.[4]

The year 1873 proved memorable for the Brothers Webb. John's arrival in Culleoka was a Godsend, and Sawney himself was deeply in love. He married Emma Clary in Unionville, Tennessee, on April 23, 1873. John stood as "security" for the couple, and J.H. Richardson was the "M.G." or officiator. Emma was the daughter of Benjamin and Alla B. Clary of Wilkesboro, North Carolina. She had attended Greensboro Female College (now Greensboro College) with Sawney's younger sister, Addie, during the Civil War, and Addie played matchmaker. The Sawney Webbs would have eight children.[5]

---

2. David P. Robbins, *Century Review of Maury County, Tennessee, 1805–1905* (Columbia, TN: Auspices of the Board of Mayor and Aldermen, 1906), 109–110.

3. McMillin, 71. Today, *The Daily Herald*, Columbia, Tennessee.

4. Parks, 261. McMillin, 72.

5. Helen C. & Timothy R. Marsh, compilers, *Official Marriages of Bedford County, Tennessee, 1861–1880, Vol. 1* (Greenville, SC: Southern Historical Press, Inc., 1996), 192. McMillin, 70, 72–73.

William Robert Webb Jr., "Son Will," the first of the eight children, was born to Sawney and Emma in 1874. They named their second son John, born in 1877, in honor of Sawney's brother and teaching partner in Culleoka.

Sawney and Emma lived in a two-story framed farmhouse just south of Culleoka across the railroad trestle over Fountain Creek and hard to the right of the railroad on a hilltop. The house featured five bedrooms with fireplaces, and the structure burgeoned with balconies. The view from the house towards Culleoka was beautiful. John had moved in with the Sawney Webbs, whose home also included student boarders. Some fourteen people lived in the house during the 1874–1875 school year. The venerable Batch, later called Sycamore Retreat, was built just across the railroad track, east of the railroad trestle, from the Sawney Webb house. It served as living quarters for boys of limited means.[6]

The year 1873 also brought a cholera epidemic that seized the South and broke up the school in Culleoka. People seldom ventured out of their homes. Sawney and Emma walked ten blocks in Nashville that fall without seeing a single person on the street. In Culleoka, with a population of about two hundred, eighteen people died in a month. The Webbs helped nurse the sick as best they could, and it was a miracle that they escaped the disease.[7]

With the school closed temporarily, John wrote to two prominent Greek professors asking to be guided in Greek for the year. One turned him down flatly, but John's letter to Prof. James Hadley of Yale University paid dividends, though Hadley had died just a few days after receiving the letter. After a long while, his son, Arthur T. Hadley, later president of Yale University, replied with the news of his father's death and also that he did not himself feel competent to guide John in the subject. He did send an outline of Greek courses offered at Yale for John's use. John would make Greek come alive for his students in Culleoka and, later, in Bell Buckle, teaching as many as eighty-one pupils in Greek one year.[8]

John Webb found his own true love in Nashville, Tennessee. He married Lily Shipp in Nashville on December 7, 1876, Methodist Bishop Holland N. McTyeire officiating. She was the daughter of Professor

6. McMillin, 77–78, 88–89.

7. Parks, 262. McMillin, 74–75.

8. McMillin, 74. McLean, 38–39.

Albert M. Shipp and his wife, Mary Jane (Gillespie) Shipp, of Vanderbilt University, but formerly of the University of North Carolina. John and Lily Webb would have five children.[9]

Professor Shipp served as dean of the Biblical department and as vice-chancellor of Vanderbilt University. John's marriage to Lily opened to John the best homes on the Vanderbilt campus, and he became a familiar and welcomed visitor among the faculty, staff, and administration.

Since arriving in Culleoka in 1873, bachelor John had lived with the Sawney Webb family; after his marriage to Lily, the couple lived for a while with his brother before moving into their own frame home in the village. By John's own count, their house was exactly "forty-five yards" downhill from the basement school in the Methodist Church, and a "downhill city block" from the new schoolhouse built in 1884. A limestone boulder in their front yard served as playground equipment for the children. John's own classroom was initially a storefront next to a saloon.[10]

John and Lily's children were born to them during the Culleoka years, the fifth child in 1886, about the time of the Bell Buckle move. Albert was born in Nashville in September 1877, Cornelia in November 1879, Mary Gillespie in October 1881, Sarah in January 1884, and Hazel Alexander in 1886.[11]

In a letter addressed to "My Dear Sister" dated January 23, 1885, from Culleoka, John writes:

> I wish you could see our children. It seems that they are all developing beautifully. I think Albert is a boy after your heart—so nimble & spry in use of feet, hands, eyes & mind—and so systematic. Mary is very bright & cunning.
>
> I spent last Friday in Mrs. Clarke's School for girls at Franklin. She has the best school for girls I know. I examined a class in Horace that did as well as our sophomore class could have done…

---

9. Ancestry.com, 2013, Webb Family Tree, Family Group Sheet, WebbArchives 1870, 148; "John Maurice Webb," Ancestry.com http://records.ancestry.com/John_Maurice_Webb_records.ashx?pid=15068514.

10. McMillin, 88–89.

11. McMillin, 87–88. "John Maurice Webb," Ancestry.com http://records.ancestry.com/John_Maurice_Webb_records.ashx?pid=15068514.

I took twenty of our boys up & we had a quotation match with as many girls. The battle was a drawn one.

Cornelia went to Nashville tonight to spend several weeks with her grandmother. Albert had a cry this evening to think of separating from her.[12]

An 1875 bulletin for Culleoka Institute included various testimonials that mentioned the preparatory school had some ninety pupils from every Southern state, and that fifty of those students were "from a distance." Six of the students were preparing for the ministry, and "the Institute is looking for some Mexican youths." It furthered stated that "What Bingham's school is to North Carolina, Webb's school is to Tennessee."

A school description of Culleoka Institute from the 1870s, signed only by Sawney Webb as "Principal," divided the curriculum between the Commercial Department, Classical Department, and Elective Studies. The Commercial Course provided a "thorough English education" intended for those not pursuing a collegiate education. It included such subjects as Bible, English, mathematics, history, geography, composition, book-keeping, reading, spelling, and penmanship. For those intending to go to college, the Classical Course included all aspects of the Commercial Course plus instruction in Greek and Latin studies, mythology, navigation and surveying, and higher mathematics, including trigonometry, analytical geometry, and calculus. Elective Studies offered French and German, natural history and philosophy, astronomy, and chemistry. The grading scale listed 50 as "excellent," winding down to 24 as "disapproved." Among the rules, regulations, and restrictions contained in the school description—and basically repeated later in the boarding system in Bell Buckle—"The pupils must become members of the Sabbath School, and attend religious services in one of the Churches every Sunday. They are forbidden to visit the village without permission, and must not be absent from their rooms at night. They must not make any store account without permission from their parents or guardians."

---

12. Webb Family Papers (Webb-Moore Papers), Southern Historical Collection, University of North Carolina, Chapel Hill, Reel 1.

Finally, student firearms were forbidden, and severe misconduct including drinking alcohol were grounds for expulsion.[13]

The 1880 census for Maury County, Tennessee, listed both John and Sawney Webb as being a "teacher in academy." John was 32, Lily, 30, Albert, 2, and daughter Cornelia was six months, having been born in November 1879. Sawney was listed as being 37, Emma, 32; Son Will, 6; Alla, 4; John, 3; and Adline, 1. Emma's mother, Alla B. Clary, 77, was living with them, as was their African American cook, nineteen-year old Ella B. Westmoreland of Alabama.[14]

The Reverend Dr. Edwin B. Chappell '74, a Culleoka graduate, wrote in *The Sunday School Magazine* for April 1927:

> I found almost nothing at Culleoka in the way of physical equipment, but I found something vastly more important than buildings and laboratories and playgrounds. In the persons of two brothers, W.R. and J.M. Webb, I found two men who taught me to despise sham and shallowness and idleness, to believe in God, in myself, in truth and integrity and justice, and in the dignity of honest work, and who awakened within me a great longing to live nobly and abundantly.

Of John, Chappell wrote: "The younger of the two brothers was one of the most inspiring and stimulating scholars and teachers I have ever met, and the contribution he made to the school was invaluable." Of Sawney, "the guiding spirit of the institution," he found in his "wisdom, insight and courageous honestly" a "kind of modern Socrates." "He drew and held his students, not by coddling them but by his unquestionable sincerity and uprightness and the power of his personality."[15]

Methodist Bishop Robert Paine of Mississippi, instrumental in the school's early growth, came to Culleoka after the first year. En route he got a splinter in his eye that became inflamed and prevented him from reading. Sawney read to him and the two became fast friends and

---

13. "From the Archives," Webb School Alumni Bulletin (Summer Edition 1975), 22. These documents are in The Webb School Archives.

14. Byron and Barbara Sistler, Preparers, *1880 Census—Tennessee, Transcription for Maury County* (Nashville, TN: B. Sistler, 1994), 61, 64.

15. McLean, 40–41.

traveling companions. Paine took a great interest in the school, sent his own grandsons to Culleoka, and encouraged many other Mississippi students to attend—the start of a large patronage from that state.[16]

A new schoolhouse with a twenty-five foot "dubious steeple" was built in 1884 for Culleoka Academy. Situated on six acres of land west of the Methodist Church, the building cost about $1,500. The frame structure resembled a thick T with two thirty-foot classrooms flanking the front entrance with an auditorium, at right angles between, thrusting some fifty feet to the rear. The entire structure sat on mortared limestone blocks, again emphasizing the "portability" of a school.

Sawney, who was building up his personal property for his growing family, had borrowed about a thousand dollars at ten percent interest, and he was out of money; it was only the timely arrival of Chief [Edmund?] McCurtain with twenty-three Choctaw boys that saved Sawney from default. Sawney chose eight of the boys, enough to fill a boarding house, for his school. Chief Curtain paid him $250 in greenbacks for each boy—$2,000—and the day was saved. Sawney had previously befriended an acquaintance of Chief McCurtain's in Louisville, who had passed the schools' circular on to Chief McCurtain.[17]

A Quarterly Report from Culleoka Institute, dated November 1, 1884, and signed "W.R. & J.M. Webb," makes for an interesting read for ten weeks of student work by one Bowdre Phinizy, a student in Culleoka and later, Bell Buckle. Mailed home to his family, the report contains no numerical grades. His Deportment is listed as "Exemplary;" English, "Excellent;" Classics, "Excellent;" and in Mathematics, "Very Respectable."

During Bowdre's first year in Culleoka, his roommate was "trapped" (a favorite classroom teaching method) by Sawney in class; the boy contended that he was right and stood up to Sawney. The disagreement escalated and the boy was finally sent home. While Bowdre was sorry to lose his roommate, he agreed that Sawney did the only thing he could do in the situation, lest the discipline of the school be undermined.[18]

16. McLean, 39. McMillin, 64.
17. Parks, 262–263. McMillin, 82–83, 87–88.
18. Benjamin Cudworth Yancey Papers, Southern Historical Collection, University of North Carolina, Chapel Hill, M-2594, Reel 12. "Trapped" refers to "Trapping," the rapid-fire game Sawney Webb employed in his classes. He learned this teaching method from his sister, Susan

Sawney Webb made his share of enemies in Culleoka, as he would again in Bell Buckle. People either loved him or hated him, but all respected him. A stern school disciplinarian, the staunch churchman and prohibitionist fought against those in Culleoka and Maury County who would sell alcohol to his students. In a time when a schoolmaster needed to be able to physically subdue an out-of-control student or even an adult, Sawney faced his enemies and found himself in at least several fistfights. Apparently, Sawney was "beaten nearly to death" in early 1886. By February, he was home in North Carolina, possibly recuperating.[19]

In a letter home dated March 21, 1886, from Culleoka, Bowdre Phinizy wrote:

> I think it will be to nearly everybody's advantage for Mr. Webb to move his school. Our John Webb is carrying on the school by himself. We have not seen Mr. Sawney Webb in two or three months. He is traveling for his health.

Bowdre added: "I think this is the best school in the country, and if I had my choice I would come here in preference to any other."[20]

In 1886, the town of Culleoka incorporated, making the sale of liquor legal within the town's limits. The saloons openly sold alcohol to students. Sawney and John Webb finally had enough. They packed up and headed to the village of Bell Buckle, Tennessee, some forty miles east on the Nashville and Chattanooga Railroad. Many of their students followed them from Culleoka, of course, emphasizing the "portability" scheme of the Binghams, and illustrating that teachers and pupils—not bricks and mortar—make a school. In Bell Buckle, another railroad town in Bedford County, the Brothers Webb would finally have a school of their own.

When the Webbs vacated Culleoka and Maury County in 1886, Culleoka Academy did not cease to exist. A number of educators succeeded them in the instruction, including both male and female teachers, right

---

("Suny"), his first teacher, and at Bingham School. Trapping is described in detail in McMillin, 103–104, and in Holliman, 287–288.

19. Rhodes Scholar Albert G. Sanders '01 to "Mr. and Mrs. McMillin," February 3, 1969, 2, The Webb School Archives. McMillin, 96.

20. Benjamin Cudworth Yancey Papers, Southern Historical Collection, University of North Carolina, Chapel Hill, M-2594, Reel 12.

up to when the Culleoka Academy building burned about 1900. Moore Institute then ensued; thereafter, Culleoka School, a public school, has occupied the site. Now K–12, the school is part of the Maury County Public Schools.

Some noted alumni of the Webb's tenure in Culleoka included: Thomas Watt Gregory '81, of Texas, Attorney General of the United States during President Woodrow Wilson's administrations from 1914 to 1919; Edward Ward Carmack '77, U.S. Senator from Tennessee; Thomas B. Lytle '86, Chancellor of the Chancery Court of Tennessee; and James A. Smiser '79, U.S. District Attorney in Alaska. While Culleoka alumni distinguished themselves in all walks of life, a goodly number entered the Christian ministry.[21]

Ned Carmack '77, a favorite of the Brothers Webb, left Culleoka to become a lawyer, newspaper editor, and U.S. Senator from Tennessee. He died tragically on the streets of Nashville on November 9, 1908, at the hands of political foes including anti-prohibitionists. Sawney Webb had the sad task of eulogizing Carmack in a memorial service in Nashville on November 15th. The service was held in what became the Ryman Auditorium, Home of Country Music, and formerly home of the Grand Ole Opry.[22]

---

21. Apparently, Culleoka lost its incorporation over the years. William Bruce Turner, *History of Maury County, Tennessee* (Nashville, TN: Parthenon Press, 1955), 92.

22. McMillin, 147–149.

Webb School and Vanderbilt University

The hand-written note was brief:

> This will introduce Willy Humphrey. He is ready for the freshman class.
> (Signed)
> William R. Webb

This was all that was needed for Willy's admission to Vanderbilt University in Nashville, Tennessee, in its early years.[1]

"The Vanderbilt" opened in the fall of 1875, with Culleoka students among its first and best students. John Webb attended the opening exercises.[2]

In his *History of Vanderbilt University* (1946), Edwin Mims refers to Webb School "whose students in the early years of Vanderbilt furnished a standard of scholarship and a type of instruction which was badly needed, especially at that time." Mims goes on:

> In 1870 W. R. Webb had come across the mountains from Bingham School to venture the foundation of a classical school modeled upon that one in North Carolina and upon others in Virginia and North Carolina. Two years later he was joined by his brother, John M. Webb, one of the best scholars who ever graduated from the University of North Carolina and who might have filled any of two or three chairs in any college or university. They made an excellent team, the one being especially strong in his effect on the morals of students and on their spiritual ideals, the other leaving a lasting impression of the discipline and elevation of scholarship. It is difficult to see how they would have succeeded if the newly established University had not from the beginning

---

1. "The Webbs of Bell Buckle," Education section, *Time* (September 16, 1946), 75.
2. McMillin, 80.

emphasized the point so well expressed by Chancellor [Landon] Garland, and it is also difficult to see how the University could have done its work without a constant flow of students from Webb's. Together these men laid the basis for the development of a large number of secondary schools in later years—schools that were founded by graduates of both institutions.

Regarding Chancellor Garland's comment, Vanderbilt University had made the decision not to have a preparatory department or school, thus classical schools like Webb and others of its type were vital to the success of Vanderbilt's program. Sawney Webb, speaking at a meeting of the National Education Association (NEA) in Louisville, Kentucky, in 1877, commented on Vanderbilt's decision not to include a preparatory wing, saying "It has brought hope to us all."

Chancellor Landon Garland said of the Webb School: "It has no superior in the Southern states."

Methodist Bishop Holland N. McTyeire (who married John Webb and his wife) of the Vanderbilt Board of Trust said of Webb School: "I know not its superior; its equal would be hard to find."[3]

Webb School sent its "oldest and best" students to Vanderbilt University in those early years. The two educational institutions were so synonymous that a Webb Old Boy won the Liars Club competition at Vanderbilt by exclaiming that he had once seen Old Sawney with his tie on straight![4]

---

3. Edwin Mims, *History of Vanderbilt University* (Nashville, TN: Vanderbilt University Press, 1946), 90–91. "Webb School" by A. Jon Frere, Headmaster of The Webb School, *The Tennessee Encyclopedia of History and Culture*, Tennessee Historical Society (Nashville, TN: Rutledge Hill Press, 1998), 1043.

4. McMillin, 80, 166.

CHAPTER FOUR

A SCHOOL OF THEIR OWN

Hoping to woo the Webb brothers to Bell Buckle to start a school, the leading citizens of the town formed a joint stock company and raised some $12,000 for the venture, a considerable sum for its day. The Webbs could use the money virtually how they pleased in establishing their school. Alfred D. Fugitt, the recognized founder of Bell Buckle, offered a beautiful six-acre plot of bluegrass and beech trees to the board of trustees for a campus at a fraction of their established value. The school would be located a third of a mile east of the depot on a hilltop along the main road through Bell Buckle.

Emma Webb's brother, Dr. William F. Clary, a graduate of Jefferson Medical College in Philadelphia, Pennsylvania, lived in Bell Buckle and agreed to serve as Webb School's doctor. He had cured Sawney Webb of tapeworm in Culleoka when big city doctors said there was no cure,

The Webb School faculty in Bell Buckle circa 1898. Seated left to right: Sawney Webb and John Webb. Standing left to right: Frank Coker, Stewart Mims, and William "Son Will" Webb.

and Sawney vowed then to move the school to Bell Buckle and include Dr. Clary in its operation.

Enticed by Bell Buckle's offer—and wanting desperately to leave Culleoka—the Brothers Webb began implementing plans for their new school, to be officially called Webb School for the first time. A newly-dug 103½-foot well provided abundant water for the new school. The Webbs designed three main buildings for the campus, spending $2,200 on the Big Room, the main schoolhouse, and $400 each for the Junior and Senior Rooms. A legal technicality forced them to leave the library at Culleoka Academy, so they spent two-thirds of the total sum, some $8,000, on books for a new library to be housed in John Webb's classroom, the Senior Room. The gentle scholar personally selected the books. The Junior Room would become Sawney's classroom where he conducted his Latin classes and recitations, though both brothers taught at times in each of

The student body in front of the Big Room in Bell Buckle in the 1890s.

the three main buildings. The first time John Andrew Rice encountered the teaching of "Old Jack," it was in the Junior Room.[1]

The buildings were built on even rows of mortared limestone pilings, following the example of the Bingham School, and again emphasizing the "portability" of a school where teachers and students were much more important than bricks and mortar.

The Big Room was a barn-like structure some 125 feet in length with Sawney Webb's gravity-defying, thirty-foot high arched entrance that belied the appearance of a livery stable. The building included a large assembly hall or auditorium in the center, some seventy feet in length with a sloping floor. A platform stood down front against the wall. There was a classroom on either side, each 40 x 25 feet, the ninth- and tenth-grade wings connected to the auditorium through large sliding doors. Two smaller rooms, both 12 x 12 cloakrooms, were attached to the rear of each classroom, and were notoriously feared as "whipping rooms" by guilty young scholars. The overall plan of the schoolhouse resembled that

1. Rice, 208.

John Webb (second row from the bottom, fourth from the left) and members of the Senior Class of 1901 in front of the Big Room in Bell Buckle.

of a "wide-winged, snub-nosed, twin-engine jet—although such a shape, like the school itself, was ahead of its time."[2]

The front of the huge structure, larger and better than the Culleoka schoolhouse and without the "dubious steeple," had four high and narrow windows on either wing and ten light-giving windows in each classroom. Again, the only brick and mortar were the chimney-wide square foundations holding the building off the ground, and there were no inside supporting posts or pillars to hide an inattentive student from the proceedings!

Built in 1886, the Big Room was utilized as the main schoolhouse until 1951, when it was demolished and replaced by the "new" Big Room, now the Sawney Webb Big Room, a modern brick edifice turned more toward Main Street (Webb Road) than the original that faced due west and was parallel to the road. The Junior Room was first moved from its original location during the construction of the new Big Room.

2. McMillin, 101.

The Senior Room and the Junior Room were nearly identical, both about 25 x 35 feet in size with high peaked-roofs and tightly fitted with horizontal clapboards of Southern longleaf pine. The roofs were covered with red cedar shingles, and each roof had a small brick chimney.

As in Culleoka, the vast majority of male students took room and board in local homes in Bell Buckle, with the few day student girls living at home. Thompson Hall, named for the first occupant of the Batch at Culleoka, was built to allow young men of limited means to save money on living expenses. A two-story box of a building with two rooms up and two below with an outdoor kitchen, the structure went up near where the Webbs were building their own homes.

In addition to the three main school buildings and Thompson Hall, apparently a few other small structures appeared on campus over time including, perhaps, a small chapel.[3]

Students at Webb School were classified based on Latin and consisted of four grades: Beginners (Freshman), Caesar (Sophomore), Junior and Senior. Each class was assigned to its own special section of the campus where the members would meet and study together sitting in their required slat-back, cane-bottomed chairs that each student toted around daily to and from class. Traditional outdoor study in the beech grove was the norm.

Each school day began with Sawney's "morning talk" in the Big Room. The faculty members, including John, waited on the main road just outside the wooden fence for Sawney to arrive. When he appeared, they stepped over the main stile in the fence to the shouts of "Over!" by scores of students, then walked over the gravel path to the Big Room. The student body would already be seated, rushing indoors and even climbing through windows to beat Sawney and the other teachers there. The bedlam of a full Big Room turned to instant silence once Sawney's party arrived, took their seats on the platform, and waited for Sawney to open the Bible. Every morning began with scripture and prayer. Then Sawney would launch into his own morning "sermon."[4]

---

3. The bulk of this section is taken from McMillin, 100–102. While the entire building was known by most of the Webb School community as the Big Room, some referred to only the auditorium portion as the Big Room.

4. Rice, 206–207.

"Trapping," a teaching method learned from sister Susan ("Suny"), Sawney and John's first teacher, and at Bingham School, was Sawney's favorite way of drilling his students. A fine line between musical chairs and a spelling bee, Sawney seated his pupils in order from ace to dunce, then began the terrifying ordeal of firing questions down the line. Any student who missed the answer had to trade places with the one who answered it correctly, and so on and so forth. "Feet on the desk, string tie awry, white-bearded Old Sawney hollered encouragement: 'Take him on it, trap him, next—next—next!'"[5]

Sawney administered justice with a beech switch usually in the principal's "office" in the thicket or in one of the coat rooms in the rear wings of the Big Room—known among the students as "whipping rooms." When a parent criticized as barbaric Sawney's use of corporal punishment as a teaching tool, the schoolmaster replied: "I'll continue to use it as long as they keep sending me young barbarians to educate."[6]

Sawney started the tradition at Webb School of announcing in morning Big Room, "You may have the day." This was an unexpected holiday given when the students had prospered in their studies and the day was particularly nice. "Then you have to move fast to get out of the way of the students," Glenn N. Holliman, a former Webb administrator and teacher remembered in the late 1970s.[7]

The Brothers Webb inspired their charges "to forsake ignorance, to be honorable, to study hard, to revere excellence, and above all, 'to never do anything on the sly.'" In tiny Bell Buckle, "the essential elements of civilization have been taught, studied, and pondered" since 1886, some 128 years.[8]

---

5. "The Webbs of Bell Buckle," Education section, *Time* (September 16, 1946), 75. For other descriptions of trapping see McMillin, 103–104, and Holliman, 287–288.

6. *Time* (September 16, 1946), 75. There is no mention of John Webb in the article.

7. "School Bells at Bell Buckle," *Southern Living* (October 1979), 44.

8. "Past is Prologue," *Webb School Alumni Directory*, 1988, vii.

The Junior Room and the Senior Room

The paint analysis performed for the 1976 restoration of the Junior Room, the sole remaining original building at The Webb School, revealed that the exterior wood siding was originally painted light tan with the doors, window frames, and roof cornices painted a light grey. The sash was a dark color, either dark brown, dark grey, black, or stained and varnished. The doors may have been painted tan with perhaps grey panels, or they could have been the color of the sash or stained and varnished. All exterior paint was oil-based. The interior of the Junior Room was simply varnished natural wood. It is assumed that the Big Room, Senior Room, and Junior Room were each constructed and painted using essentially the same building materials, and that the interiors of each building were natural wood with a light coating of varnish.[1]

When John Andrew Rice '08 arrived on campus as a new student in 1905, the already decaying buildings had turned a deep brown. With successive paintings over time, economy and availability of paint materials would produce buildings painted a kind of battleship gray and, finally, "church white." The chosen 1976 restoration color for the Junior Room was a yellow buff with gray trimmings. Also at the time of restoration, the Junior Room had a metal roof. "We thought it always had a metal roof," Glenn N. Holliman reported. "But we found that originally the roof had been wooden shingles. That's what was found under the metal."[2]

---

1. "Paint Analysis of the Junior Room, Webb School, Bell Buckle, Tennessee," August 1976, by Building Conservation Technology, Inc., and submitted to Architect-Engineer Associates, Inc., Nashville, Tennessee. Project funded by a matching grant from the Department of the Interior under the National Historic Preservation Act of 1966. Webb School, Junior Room, Development Project # 477600129-00. Funding for the restoration was also provided by "the generous alumni of Webb School," and the project was directed and supervised by the Tennessee Historical Commission (Holliman, 288).

2. Max York, "They've Saved Sawney's Room," *The Tennessean* (Sunday, November 27, 1977), 1–2 F ("Panorama").

The 1894 Webb School Tigers football team. The Senior Room, the classroom of John Webb and the original school library, sits in the background along the Main Road through Bell Buckle.

Both the Junior Room and Senior Room featured ten, ten-foot high and three feet wide windows—three windows on each side and two windows each both front and back. In the age before electric lights, the Webb brothers sought to utilize as much natural light as possible. The front of the Junior Room included a door on the left side with two windows evenly-spaced to the right of the door. The back door was centered with a window on each side. The Senior Room differed in that the front door was centered with a window on each side, and the back of the building originally included two windows evenly-spaced and no back door! In time, steps were added to the back window to the right, and a small door was later cut to the right of that window. Sitting on open limestone pilings where the wind and cold, animals, and even students could crawl under and through, lattice work was later placed around the pilings

The Junior Room, the classroom of Sawney Webb, in its original location in Bell Buckle circa 1906

of all three buildings, with the outer pilings exposed, for both aesthetic, hygienic, and safety purposes. The Junior Room sat just behind the Big Room to the southeast, while the Senior Room "with the exciting new library at one end" was built on the knoll beside the main road in the northwest corner of the campus. Each classroom was warmed by a pot-bellied stove which provided adequate heat mainly to those sitting directly in front or around it; and the Big Room, with the 9th graders on one side and the 10th graders on the other, was warmed by two pot-bellied stoves.[3]

---

3. Holliman, 287–293, 304. McMillin, 100–103. Bowdre Phinizy '88 mentioned three pot-bellied stoves for 180 students in the Big Room in a letter home dated January 2, 1887. Randolph Elliott (Ida A. Elliott) in the article, "Old Sawney's," in *The Atlantic Monthly* (August 1920), 232, remembered one "huge cast-iron stove in the middle" of the building.

Inside each classroom—the Junior Room could hold upwards of seventy students sitting on hard wooden benches and hickory, cane-bottomed chairs—a wooden desk or lectern on a raised dais was provided for the teacher. While it has been assumed that the side walls were painted black for use as chalkboards, the paint analysis for the 1976 restoration of the Junior Room did not bear this out. "The configuration of the wall siding itself seems to rule out the possibility of writing directly on the wall surface. It is quite likely, however, that separate blackboards, either painted wood or slate, were hung on the walls." Invariably, the weather dictated whether the teacher and students needed to sit as close to the heated pot-bellied stove as possible. In warm or hot weather, the doors and large windows could be open for ventilation but, while shades were provided to block the sun, none of the windows had screens in those days. Both Sawney and John Webb liked to tilt their chairs while teaching, Sawney propping his feet on the stove.[4]

The three main buildings were "mellowed by almost a half a century to a deep brown, with cracks under and around doors and windows through which the wind blew serenely cold on a winter day. Pot-bellied stoves, heated red-hot, shed warmth for at most five feet," remembered John Andrew Rice '08.[5] Vermont Royster's first impression of Bell Buckle and Webb School in 1929 was that of a "ghost town," and he was surprised that the clapboard buildings proved to be classrooms with pot-bellied stoves! Royster '31, the Pulitzer Prize-winning editor of *The Wall Street Journal*, quickly learned that this ghost town had a real ghost: "Dead these three years, Old Sawney Webb stalked the classrooms, the Big Room and the playing fields, tie askew, coattails flapping, as tangible and real as if he were alive."[6]

4. Richard G. Tune, Assistant Director for National Register Program, Tennessee Historical Commission, Department of Conservation, Nashville, Tennessee, to author, October 25, 1989. "Junior Room," no author and unpaged. "Specifications For Restoration of Webb School Junior Room, Project No. 47-76-00129-00, October 6, 1976," presented by Architect-Engineer Associates, Nashville, Tennessee.

5. Rice, 202.

6. "Foreword," Vermont Royster '31, McMillin, xi, xii.

The Senior Room, John Webb's classroom and the original school library, was hard by the main road passing east-west through Bell Buckle (Main Street, now Webb Road, East). The classroom and library were protected by the wooden fence with its many boy-built stiles which ran the length of the school property. With the advent of the automobile, a section of the fence was removed so that cars could pull off the road and park directly in front of the Senior Room.[7] The beloved Senior Room, which was never moved, was torn down in 1927 to make way for a sign of the times, a parking lot. The site of the Senior Room, unmarked today, was about where the (Edwin McNeill) Poteat Memorial Gates are currently located, once the entrance to the parking lot. "Son Will" Webb would later build his handsome home directly across the road from the Senior Room.[8]

John Webb selected an excellent collection of books for the school's library and his classroom. The library was opened to any and all who wished to avail themselves of its treasures, whether or not they were connected to Webb School. The books were available free to all. "The 'Senior Room,' in which they were housed, was his classroom, and he taught surrounded by the books he loved, which were themselves testimonials to his scholarly attainments. From him students caught a love for good literature, as well as for Latin and Greek, for he guided them in the selection of what they were to read and taught them to appreciate the great masterpieces." As John Webb once wrote: "You must go to sources to find what a man really thought and believed; you cannot take the labels of men." John Andrew Rice wrote: "…The books were not adolescent nor for adolescents; for he knew the young want to grow. He chose mainly what he liked to read himself, and they were put on the shelves in

---

7. A snapshot in The Webb School Archives shows an automobile parked in front of the Senior Room, circa 1923. Old Boys Alfred Farrar '19 and Jack Chambers '24 stand in the foreground.

8. For the Poteat Gates, see "New School Entrance" in *The Oracle*, the Webb School newspaper, Vol. 5, No. 1 (October 1942), 1. Son Will's "gracious two-storied, large white wood framed house burned in 1971. Prior to 1900, the site was part of Sawney's farm. After the 1971 fire, the ruins were bulldozed and the grounds landscaped and seeded with grass." "Junior Room," 2–3.

some spiritual order that would make a student of 'library science' shudder. The *Origin of Species* might sit between the poems of Keats and Lane's *Latin Grammar* and be none the worse for the company. He was no Aristotelian; he knew the limits and poison of classification." The gentle scholar supervised the selection of new books for the school library until his death in 1916.[9]

The John Webb Library would be built beginning in 1927, and dedicated at commencement in 1928 during a reunion of the Class of 1903. A memorial to the class through the generosity of J. Russell Simpson '03 of Tulsa, Oklahoma, the 42' x 63' building of mat brick and stone construction, roofed with red tile, cost some $20,000 of donated money. Shortly after the reunion, the "books were removed from the simple structure which had sheltered them for over forty years and placed in the new building." Like the Senior Room, it was opened to the general public in addition to the Webb School family, the John Webb Library being the only public library in Bedford County for many years. "The quality of its books is its chief claim to distinction," wrote David N. McQuiddy, Webb School's librarian in the 1930s, the collection then containing over 8,000 select volumes and ranking "first in size among the private school libraries of the South." The books were catalogued via the Dewey Decimal System by librarian Alla Webb, and the Library of Congress card service was implemented.[10] Sawney Webb always maintained that "the purpose of an education is to teach one to read," and both the selection of books and overall improvement of the John Webb Library became an active life-long interest of William R. Webb Jr., "Son Will," as he shepherded Webb School through trying times

---

9. McQuiddy, 3, reprint (see below). Rice, 213–214. Mims, 11. McMillin, 134–135. David N. McQuiddy, Librarian, The Webb School, Bell Buckle, "The Webb School Library," *The Tennessee Teacher*, The Tennessee Education Association, Vol. 3, No. 9 (May, 1936), 40–44. One of Webb School's "great teachers," David McQuiddy was raised in Bell Buckle and educated at Webb, Vanderbilt (Phi Beta Kappa), and Chicago. He later served as the long-time headmaster of Tennessee Military Institute in Sweetwater, Tennessee. McQuiddy was a pallbearer at Sawney Webb's funeral in 1926. See "David N. McQuiddy, 1902-1987," *The Webb School Magazine* (Fall 1988), 21–22.

10. McQuiddy, 3–5, reprint.

in successive decades.[11] The former John Webb Library is today utilized by the history department.

The Junior Room, listed on the National Register of Historic Places, is Webb School's surviving example of a "portable" schoolroom. Since its construction in 1886, it has occupied four different locations on campus: its original location southeast of the Big Room and near the later John Webb Library (1927); an obscure site on the southwest corner of the campus (about where the Bradley A/V Building is located today) where it became the Platonic Debating Society Room—moved there because of the construction of the new modern brick Big Room in 1952; its most prominent and picturesque site after restoration in 1976 among the stately maple and oak trees in front of Chambliss Dorm (boys), about where the Son Will home stood for some seventy years (circa 1900–1971), and where the Austin Davis-Bryant Woosley Computer/Science Center now stands; and, finally, the Junior Room's present location between the Son Will Building (1927; Admissions) and the new Student Center (the Puryear Building being moved to accommodate its construction). Utilized over the years for a variety of usages including as a classroom, study hall, art studio, and school museum (nearly always unlocked), the Junior Room is again used as a classroom and is usually locked when not in use. The covered front and back porches of the Junior Room—an addition in later years while sitting in its original location—detracts from the original plan of the Junior Room and its impeccable restoration in 1976 supervised by the Tennessee Historical Commission.[12]

Around 1960, for insurance purposes, the Junior Room was named the George Beale Building, after a beloved teacher who taught at Webb in the early 1890s.[13] As of 2000, the John B. Hardin '50 Endowment maintains the Junior Room for posterity.

11. McQuiddy, 1–3, reprint.

12. At least several images (circa 1920s–1940s) in The Webb School Archives show the covered front porch of the Junior Room in its original location fronting what was then the athletic field. Apparently, the rear entrance was also covered.

13. "Junior Room," 2–3.

Bowdre Phinizy, Class of 1888

Bowdre Phinizy studied under the Webbs in Culleoka (1884–1886) and in Bell Buckle (1886–1888), before entering Princeton University. He later enjoyed a distinguished career as a journalist and newspaper owner in Georgia, his home state. A number of his student letters from Culleoka and Bell Buckle are included in the Benjamin Cudworth Yancey Papers, Southern Historical Collection, University of North Carolina, Chapel Hill. The letters are usually addressed to his grandmother or mother, and frequently mention the Webbs.

Phinizy's letters provide a fascinating account of life as a boarding student: trapping and debating and winning a "distinction;" revivals and converting; student speeches and recitations; eating lots of popped corn and ice cream; and getting the mail twice daily as the trains ran to and from Nashville past Culleoka and Bell Buckle. The following descriptive entries are all from letters Bowdre Phinizy sent home from Bell Buckle that are contained in Microfilm Reels 12 and 13 of the Benjamin Cudworth Yancey Papers, Southern Historical Collection, Louis Round Wilson Special Collections Library, University of North Carolina, Chapel Hill:

Reel 12 (Selected passages)

August 31, 1886: Bowdre is thrilled to be assigned by Mr. [Sawney] Webb to the best boarding house in town, and he relates that "Both of the Messrs. Webb are well etc."

September 19, 1886: "Mr. Webb is very strict and is often cross, but I suppose we do many things to vex him. I can't get over my objections to sulphur water. It is very strong."

"The creamery affords us as much ice cream as we can eat. I have been patronizing it a little too freely I am afraid. But the cream is so nice."

October 13, 1886: On letterhead, "Webb School, A Classical Training School for Boys, Bell Buckle, Tenn.," Bowdre writes: "We have a splendid library, but I have not any time to read except Friday night & Saturday, and I like to play too well so don't read as much as I want to."

November 14, 1886: "Our school…will be a splendid success as long as 'Old Sawney' is at the helm. We are just closing a series of meetings at the school-house. About 27 boys were converted and nine today joined the Methodist church. So I think the meeting a brilliant success, and we ought to be encouraged."

Reel 13 (Selected passages)
January 2, 1887: "The weather is intensely cold. The coldest we had this weather. It is a hard time we have keeping warm. So many boys around a small fire. We will have little comfort at the school-house this cold weather. The school-house is very poorly heated. Only three stoves and 180 boys. Over 50 boys to a stove is not comfortable."

January 23, 1887: "Belle Buckle is in quite a 'boom.' The railroad is going to erect a passenger depot, and houses both private and stores are being erected all over the place. Both of the Messrs. Webb are having handsome buildings [homes] erected."

"Our library is still increasing and I hope before long we shall have two or three thousand volumes."

January 5 & February 23, 1887: "Every two weeks Mr. [Sawney] Webb takes the number of distinctions each boarding-house has made and divides the number of distinctions by the number of boys and places the record on the blackboard. Our house is leading this two weeks. The majority of the boys in my house are new ones and all of them are very small in size. So I think we deserve praise for leading the school."

January 30, 1887: "The Messrs. Webb think that there is no Southern man of such promise as Grady [Henry W. Grady (1850–1889), "Spokesman of the New South"], and I do too."

Bowdre's letter includes references to fishing, food, baseball, and Bell Buckle's ice cream parlor and soda-water fountain.

February 6, 1887: "Friday night the Platonic Society conferred upon me the honor of Public Secretary."

"I was reading a Harvard catalogue a few days ago and if Mother approves I would like to go there after I finish Mr. Webb's course. Two boys besides myself are thinking of going from here to Harvard and it would be very pleasant to go with them. Both of them are in my class. I think it is best to go to the best college when you go to one so I prefer Harvard to Athens [Georgia] or any southern institution."

"My Junior class has just commenced the Fasti of Ovid and I like them very much. Mr. [Sawney] Webb makes every thing as clear and plain as usual and I still think as a school-master he has no equal."

May 22, 1887: Near the close of school... "Every day some homesick boy makes a calculation of the days, hours, min and second before he shall leave for home, and puts the result upon the blackboard in a conspicuous place. Every body is thinking about home and none more than myself."

October 23, 1887: Now a senior, Bowdre Phinizy was chosen from the student body to receive the president of the United States and his lady [Grover Cleveland and his wife, Frances Folsom Cleveland] when their train stopped briefly in Bell Buckle. Bowdre had his speech prepared and was ready to introduce selected students. However, the train did not stop and just sped right on by. While it appears that the assembled throng at least had a glance of the president, everyone was certainly disappointed.

Bowdre becomes a willing participant in the bicycling craze sweeping the country.

November 19, 1887: "Last night, Gov. [Robert Love] Taylor of Tennessee [a noted fiddler] spoke to the school and also expounded on music."

"Our school has been especially favored of late. We have a glance both of the Pres. and of state gov."

Bowdre turned sixteen on December 27th.

December 3, 1887: The students did not get off for Thanksgiving, but classes did let out a little early.

"Mr. [Sawney] Webb gives as is his custom only one day X-mas. Since X-mas is on Sunday he proposed to give us Monday in its stead."

January 13, 1888: "Our class will soon begin the study of German. I don't think that in the five months that we are here we will make much progress, tho we will have a splendid teacher, Mr. John Webb. In all of our college we are oblige to know either German or French, that is to have some knowledge of the language for admittance."

March 10, 1888: Bowdre will deliver an oration fairly soon at Webb [Commencement?] and has sent a copy of his speech to his grandfather, Benjamin C. Yancey, for editing. He has received it back with comments to improve the speech for delivery.

CHAPTER FIVE

BELL BUCKLE,
HOME OF WEBB SCHOOL

Bell Buckle in northern Bedford County, Tennessee, lies some fifty miles southeast of Nashville and some eighteen miles southeast of Murfreesboro. It is fifteen miles northeast of Shelbyville, and some one hundred miles northwest of Chattanooga. Bell Buckle lies within the Upper Duck River Valley watershed. Shelbyville is the county seat of Bedford County, an area featuring beautiful landscapes of rolling hills and flat open vistas.

One of a number of railroad towns created when the Nashville and Chattanooga (and later St. Louis) Railroad bed was laid connecting Nashville, Chattanooga, Atlanta, and points east, Bell Buckle was founded as the third town in the county by Alfred D. Fugitt, a local landowner and farmer. Named for Bell Buckle Creek, one version is that the name was derived from a local legend that Cherokee Indians killed a cow of a farmer by a spring and tacked the cow's bell and buckle on a tree as a warning.[1]

Sporting a bank (later two banks) and a hotel with a "booming" population of upwards to 1,000 people by the time the Webb families arrived in 1886, the village would combine local manufacturing and commercial businesses with notable educational opportunities and refined living in well-appointed homes characteristic of mid to late nineteenth-century America.

The main line of the Nashville and Chattanooga Railroad was being laid in the area in 1852, stimulating growth. Alfred Fugitt donated land for the railroad and depot, and opened the town's first general store in 1852. A brick railroad depot was built in 1853, and the town of Bell Buckle was incorporated in 1856. The village became a major railroad stockyard between Nashville and Chattanooga. During the Civil War, Bell Buckle figured prominently in the Tullahoma Campaign of 1863.

On Monday, June 1, 1863, Confederate Lieutenant General William J. Hardee reviewed Brigadier General St. John R. Liddell's Arkansas Brigade in "Bellbuckle." Accompanying Hardee and his staff was a British military officer on furlough, Lieutenant Colonel Arthur James Lyon Fremantle of H.M. Coldstream Guards, who recorded the event in his travel diary.

Describing both the weather and the scenery as "delightful," Fremantle viewed Liddell's troops as "five very weak regiments which had suffered severely in the different battles…" He related that "before the marching past of the brigade, many of the soldiers had taken off their coats and marched past the general in their shirt sleeves, on account of the warmth. Most of them were armed with Enfield rifles captured from the enemy. Many, however, had lost or thrown away their bayonets, which they don't appear to value properly, as they assert that they have never met any Yankees who would wait for that weapon." Finally, "They drilled tolerably well, and an advance in line was remarkably good; but General Liddell had invented several dodges of his own, for which he was reproved by General Hardee."[2]

1. The spring is reportedly located just south of the Lynch House Hotel at the foot of Hinkle Hill in Bell Buckle.

2. Walter Lord, *Editing and Commentary, The Fremantle Diary, Being the Journal of Lieutenant Colonel Arthur James Lyon Fremantle, Coldstream Guards, On His Three Months in the Southern*

Bell Buckle played a major role in the nearby Liberty Gap engagement of June 24–26, 1863, a site several miles north of Bell Buckle along Liberty Pike, which is today State Route 269. One of several gaps in the Highland Rim that were strategic to both armies during the Tullaholma Campaign, the battle was fought in miserable weather with incessant rain and mud as the Confederate Army of Tennessee under General Braxton Bragg fought a delaying action against the Union advance of General William S. Rosecrans. Liddell's Arkansas brigade of Confederate Major General Patrick Cleburne's division formed a position near the town after being driven out of the pass. The Confederates then formed for an attack on the Federal troops holding the gap on June 25th, only to be repulsed and driven back nearly a mile. The Tullahoma Campaign resulted in Bragg's retreat from the valley of the Duck River and the loss of Middle Tennessee to Rosecrans.[3]

After the war, the village featured a large creamery, a milling company, and a small shovel making factory. A freight depot had been built along the double railroad track with the stockyard adjoining.

The greatest period of prosperity for Bell Buckle occurred after about 1870, and the village was experiencing a "boomlet" when the Brothers Webb arrived to start their classical school in 1886. Bell Buckle soon became "a cattle town with intellectual sophistication. Here a parrot recited Greek and a cow caught mistakes in Latin," wrote Laurence McMillin in *The Schoolmaker*.[4]

Similar to Culleoka, fire destroyed much of the original "square" in Bell Buckle during the 1890s; many of the existing buildings date from that period.

States (Boston, MA: Little, Brown and Company, 1954), 123–125. Fremantle's extraordinary journey through the Confederacy took him from Brownsville, Texas, to Mobile, Alabama, up to Shelbyville and Wartrace, Tennessee (where he spent a week with the Army of Tennessee), back down to Chattanooga, Tennessee, and Atlanta, Georgia, then over to Charleston, South Carolina, up to Richmond, Virginia, and finally up to the battlefield of Gettysburg, Pennsylvania, where he witnessed the three-day slaughter of Americans by accompanying General Robert E. Lee's Army of Northern Virginia.

3. "The Tullahoma Campaign – Communities – Bell Buckle." http://mtweb.mtsu.edu/tullproj/Communities/bell_buckle.html; Tennessee Civil War Preservation Association (TCWPA), "The Civil War in Rutherford and Bedford Counties." http://www.tcwpa.org/the-civil-war-in-rutherford-and-bedford-counties.

4. McMillin, 9.

The First World War, followed by the economic downturn leading to the Great Depression, devastated Bell Buckle and its railroad trade. The population fell sharply by 1924 to 500 inhabitants.[5]

---

5. Legend, 1924 Sanborn Fire Maps of Bell Buckle, Tennessee.

CHAPTER SIX

"GOD IS OFTEN PLEASED BUT NEVER SATISFIED"
—George MacDonald (1824–1905)

As the Big Room and the Senior and Junior Rooms were being built for occupancy with the opening of school in August 1886, the homes of Sawney and John Webb were also under construction, though it appears that work on their private homes continued into early 1887. Perhaps both families stayed at the Lynch Hotel in Bell Buckle temporarily while waiting to move into their new homes.

The John Webb house on the west side of Maple Street was a two-and-a-half story display of Victorian tracery built in the Queen Anne style, a true "painted lady" with chimneys on the north and south sides of the home. Painted buff-colored or light green with dark green shutters, the house had a small front porch with a long porch and balcony on the north side. The bedrooms were upstairs, and the parlor, dining room, pantry, and John's beloved study and library were downstairs. There was a large opening in the center of the house with the staircase and a large

The John Webb house on the west side of Maple Street in Bell Buckle. (Postcard courtesy of the Bedford County Historical Society, Shelbyville TN)

"base-burner, round with isenglass in the upper part in which anthracite coal was burned in colder weather. This stove must have heated well the second floor as well as the ground floor. There were many trees, mostly maples, especially at the rear of the house." Finally, there was at least one small building immediately to the rear of the house, probably the kitchen.[1]

John's private library, his personal sanctuary, grew to "seven or eight thousand or even more" books, overflowing his well-appointed study, spilling into the hallways, and eventually engulfing the whole of the house including the attic. The books, later double-stacked throughout the house, reached from floor to ceiling. In nearly all of his books, John wrote his name and sometimes the date of acquisition. Of course, he always shared his books with anyone who had an interest in a particular title or subject, from family members and the students to the community at large.[2]

1. Long letter to "Mr. and Mrs. Laurence McMillin" from Albert G. Sanders, Jackson, Mississippi, February 3, 1969, typescript with transcription in The Webb School Archives; McMillin, 135.

2. Mims, 22. McMillin, 135. The John Webb home burned in May 1935. It was sold along with other properties in Bell Buckle following John's death in April 1916, when the family vacated Bell Buckle and Webb School for good. In November, 1918, the Mullins family moved into the home and lived there until it burned. Information and a snapshot of the house when the Mullins

"GOD IS OFTEN PLEASED BUT NEVER SATISFIED"   55

The John Webb family had a beautiful white and brown setter named Spica, Latin for thorn, as Lily's brother, Thornwell Shipp, had given them the dog. Spica always barked furiously at passersby from the front yard until the carriage gate was opened; then, he suddenly lost his courage and retreated! This was always a constant source of laughter for John and the family. Spica was certainly no match for Sydney across the street, the enormous Saint Bernard of the Sawney Webb family.[3]

Life was good for the John Webb family in Bell Buckle, if not lonely for both John and Lily for want of cultural and intellectual stimulation. Their children were devoted to them and enjoyed happy relationships with Sawney and Emma's children, their cousins, across the street. John loved tending to his garden, and Lily, as refined and cultivated as any Southern belle, enjoyed playing the quintessential hostess, entertaining

family lived there was provided this author by James D. Mullins of Battle Creek, Michigan, and Jim and Dorothy (Mullins) Crenshaw of Murfreesboro, Tennessee. Dorothy was born in the John Webb home.

3. Sanders letter to the McMillins, February 3, 1969.

The 1897–98 Webb School Tennis Club posed in the yard of the John Webb house. Daughters of both John and Sawney Webb are included in this group. The dog is Spica, the family dog of the John Webb family.

the elite of Southern academic circles in her well-kept pastoral home. Guests included President Woodrow Wilson of Princeton, President Francis Venable of Chapel Hill (Son Will's brother-in-law), Chancellor James Kirkland of Vanderbilt, and Vice-Chancellor Benjamin Wiggins of Sewanee, among many others. Lily's parlor, decorated in mahogany and oriental rugs, reflected her impeccable taste, and her table boasted the finest greaseless chicken that one could eat with white kidd gloves.[4]

Years later when asked how she entertained Woodrow Wilson in her Maple Street home, Lily replied: "Entertain Mr. Wilson! He entertained himself and everybody else in the room. There's no trouble about entertaining Mr. Wilson."[5]

While discussing racial matters at dinner one evening, Lily Webb remarked regarding Booker T. Washington's newly published autobiography *Up From Slavery* (1901): "I would not object to having Booker Washington sitting at this table with us," to which the others fairly nodded in agreement.[6]

Politically, John Webb considered himself an Independent Democrat.

John and Lily enjoyed long walks about the village, and the whole family embraced the bicycling fad of the 1890s, taking every opportunity to ride whenever the roads were passable. John even threatened to ride his bicycle all the way to North Carolina if the roads were good.[7]

John was not above quoting someone, known or unknown, and he often repeated a quote by the Scottish writer and Christian minister, George MacDonald: "God is often pleased but never satisfied." It became something of his mantra in life.[8]

The gentle scholar was actually made president of the Bank of Bell Buckle. Ever practical with a good head for business which he openly

---

4. McMillin, 137–138.

5. Sanders letter to the McMillins, February 3, 1969. As reported by Glenn N. Holliman in his article, "The Webb School Junior Room, The Symbol of a School," in *Tennessee Historical Quarterly*, Vol. 36, No. 3 (Fall 1977), 299, James G. Alley, Webb School Class of 1909, said that one of Woodrow Wilson's daughters vacationed for several weeks with one of John and Lily Webb's daughters in Bell Buckle. The visit was probably in 1908 or 1909. From a quote by Lily Webb included later in this work, it appears that Margaret Woodrow Wilson was that daughter.

6. Sanders letter to the McMillins, February 3, 1969.

7. McMillin, 137.

8. Rice, 218.

"GOD IS OFTEN PLEASED BUT NEVER SATISFIED"   57

The Sawney Webb house on the east side of Maple Street in Bell Buckle circa 1906

shared with family and friends, John managed to build up a tidy portfolio of securities for his own family.[9]

Sawney and Emma Webb's house was directly across Maple Street from John and Lily's. Much larger than the John Webb home, the massive two-story Victorian (if not Roman) structure featured a wide front porch supported by various matching pairs of Ionic pillars. The frame house was originally painted a beige color which later gave way to "church white." Sawney's book-lined office, always open, was accessed through a special

---

9. McMillin, 137. The bank no longer exists, but its vault with small wall safe survives and is on display in Hilltop Antiques, which presently occupies the site of the bank. The Bank of Bell Buckle was organized in 1887, and incorporated in 1889. With the Stock Market Crash and the onset of the Great Depression, the bank liquidated on December 31, 1931, paying depositors 25½% of their assets. The 43-year old bank succumbed to the town's declining population and economic resources. The other bank, The People's Bank and Trust Company of Bell Buckle, was established in 1909. This bank liquidated in 1926, the year of Sawney Webb's death, paying depositors 30% of their assets. The bank with its covered porch sat next to the Lynch House Hotel across Main Street from the surviving business block. The empty bank building was damaged by a tank which ran into it during Army maneuvers during the period of World War II. See David R. Beavers, *A History of Banks of Bedford County, Tennessee, 1807–1983*, privately printed (October 1987), 23–24. Holliman, 301.

side entrance, and the attic served two generations of family members as a roller skating rink during inclement weather. Sawney and Emma loved to relax on their spacious porch which became a center of activity for their large family. Built in 1886–1887, Sawney moved his family in during the summer of 1887. Their home normally included student boarders. Much later, the vacated house would be used as a boy's dormitory called Sawney Webb Hall or just Sawney Hall. The house was also the first girl's dormitory when the school's boarding program went coed in 1973. The venerable old landmark was struck by lightning and completely destroyed by fire in 1982. In all, the house served as a dormitory from about 1940-1980. Sawney's barn and corncrib, built on a plan somewhat similar to that of the Senior and Junior Rooms, burned in 2006.[10]

Rhodes Scholar Albert G. Sanders '01 remembered that his uncle, John Webb, had a nervous affliction, reportedly brought about due to strain caused when Sawney was "beaten nearly to death" in Culleoka, and the school was entrusted to John's singular care for perhaps several months. John harbored strange little peculiarities: he would not touch a cup of coffee if some had spilled in the saucer. His daughters could not wear stripped dresses as it reminded him of convict wear. He could not endure the Negro spiritual, "Couldn't Hear Nobody Pray," as he heard a Negro singing it in jail at midnight. He never went overseas to Europe or elsewhere as he could not stand a wide body of open water. Depression came upon him in springtime, and Sawney would travel with him in the mountains. Through it all, John maintained his sense of humor and his gentleness to all. He could be stern, as his children could attest, but not often.

Sanders never saw John conduct morning chapel. When in charge on Sunday afternoons, John would simply read some good story or other piece of literature to the students.[11]

The Webb families were members of the Methodist Episcopal [M.E.] Church, South, in Bell Buckle (now the Bell Buckle United Methodist Church). Located on the east side of Maple Street just down from the homes of Sawney and John Webb, the church was founded in 1807, and

10. McMillin, 105, 143–144. *Postcard Memories of Bedford County, Tennessee.* Bicentennial Celebration 2007, Published by the Bedford County Historical Society, Shelbyville, Tennessee (Nashville, TN: Panacea Press, 2006), 134.

11. Sanders letter to the McMillins, February 3, 1969.

the present church building was built in 1893 (and renovated in 1995) at the insistence of Sawney Webb and the pastor then, Reverend T.J. Duncan. They wanted a close relationship between the church and Webb School, a strong association still maintained today. The Webb families contributed to the construction of a new sanctuary for the church during the booming 1890s, and John Webb taught a Sunday School class and assisted the young pastors-in-training.[12]

A delightful story involves the young preacher sent by his church conference to pastor the Bell Buckle church. Coming into John Webb's presence, discussing theology with the gentle scholar and perusing John's outstanding personal library rich in religious tomes, the young preacher had "the light shone upon him." He startled the congregation one Sunday morning by announcing that unless there was sickness and distress among the congregation, to which he would certainly respond, he would not be calling on church members. He simply had too much work to do in his study![13]

As the Webb School program grew and improved, student activities solidified.

The Webb Summer School (Camp) was organized in 1898 and ran until 1938. It was located at Walling, Tennessee, on the Caney Fork River near Rock Island and McMinnville. Teacher Edward T. Price '00, Sawney's son-in-law, initially directed the summer camp. Thompson Webb '07, one of Sawney's sons then studying at Chapel Hill, was "instructor in charge" at least during the summer of 1911. The summer school letterhead listing Thompson also included unique "Uncle Remus" characters. The present summer school program at The Webb School was begun in 1975. Glenn N. Holliman directed the summer school from 1975 to 1981.[14]

The Young Men's Christian Association (Y.M.C.A.) was popular both on the Webb campus and with Webb alumni in Nashville. Sawney Webb, for one, was a great supporter of the Y.M.C.A.

---

12. Mildred Locke, compiler and writer, *Bell Buckle United Methodist Church—100 Years, 1883-1993*. Est. 1807, privately printed, 10–11.

13. Mims, 22. McMillin, 136.

14. Holliman, 299, 301. The 1911 Summer School flyer is in The Webb School Archives. Email to the author from Glenn N. Holliman dated November 5, 2013.

At least by 1907, Webb School organized a small school orchestra to play for functions at the school and locally.

The 50th Annual Public Debate of the Hamilton & Platonic Debating Societies was held at the school on Tuesday evening, June 2, 1925. Debate had been an integral part of the educational program from the very beginning of Webb School, the debaters themselves being popular with the student body. Most debaters were among the top students in the school.

Athletics, too, were always a vital part of the Webb School program. Baseball, football, basketball, and tennis were popular sports played both in clubs and intramurals and, later, as varsity teams competing with outside opponents.

On August 25, 1888, the Brothers Webb wrote the following recommendation for Edwin Mims '88:

> This is to certify that Edwin Mims was a pupil of ours for several terms and has received honorable discharge. He is worthy of the confidence of any institution he may seek to enter.
>
> (Signed)
> W.R. and J.M. Webb,
> Princ.'s Webb School.

Edwin Mims decided to go to Vanderbilt University.[15]

Dr. Edwin Mims was John Webb's protégé and academic "son." From his school days at Webb School until John's death in 1916, Mims remained a close friend and confidant of the gentle scholar.

When Edwin was pursuing graduate work in English, John Webb surprised him by often guiding him better in his study than some his university professors. Mims remembered: "Many were the talks that we had on Wordsworth, Tennyson, and Browning at a time when I was just discovering them."[16]

Sawney, Son Will, and two Culleoka alumni toured Europe in the summer of 1889, Sawney leaving the school in John Webb's charge.

---

15. Letter of reference, August 25, 1888, Box 16, Webb Correspondence, Edwin Mims Papers, Vanderbilt University, Nashville, Tennessee.

16. Mims, 13. McMillin, 135.

John was suddenly "seized with a serious illness and spent the summer in a sanitarium." The news of John's nervous breakdown did not reach Sawney in Europe in a timely manner, and upon his return and learning about John, Sawney feared that he no longer had a school with which to support his family. Amazingly, according to Emma Webb McLean '02, Sawney's wife, Emma, had taken charge of the situation. Aided by R. Grier Peoples '83, one of the assistant teachers, she "engaged" and registered some 200 boys, and secured an excellent faculty for the school year including hiring one new teacher – just the faculty that Sawney had wanted![17]

A favorite stop for Sawney and Son Will during their European trip was a tour of Eton College, arguably the most famous school for boys in the world. Located just across the Thames River from Windsor Castle, the alumni rolls of this English public school (private) read like a who's who of world history, including both the famous and the infamous. Sawney and Son Will marveled that the school's furniture and even its own "Big Room" were no better than what they had at Webb School. English aristocrats wanted their sons to learn to withstand hardship, thus their Eton experience was Spartan, at best. When Sawney asked the proctor who was showing them around, "If I should leave my son here, what would it cost, sir?," the proctor replied: "Are you a gentleman, sir?" Sawney responded: "In my country, everyone is assumed to be a gentleman, unless he proves otherwise, sir."[18]

William Robert Webb Jr., Son Will '91 (1874–1960), began teaching at Webb in 1897 after receiving his degree Phi Beta Kappa from the University of North Carolina and teaching English there. He had been educated at Webb School and at Phillips Academy in Andover, Massachusetts, before going to Chapel Hill. Son Will became a principal with his father and uncle in 1908, and later led the school as sole head until his retirement in 1952.

Son Will married Louise H. Manning, daughter of North Carolina Congressman and UNC law professor, John Manning, Jr. Her sister, Sally Charleton, became the wife of Francis P. Venable, president of the

17. McLean, 33–34. McMillin, 106–108.

18. McMillin, 106–107. Of course, Prince William, Duke of Cambridge, and Prince Harry of Wales are two of the most famous recent Etonians.

University of North Carolina, making Son Will and Venable brothers-in-law, and Francis Venable a noted visitor to Bell Buckle and Webb School.[19]

Gerald Webb Follin Sr. '08 (1891–1962) began teaching English at Webb in 1914. For thirty-two years he served as Son Will's assistant principal, becoming principal in 1952 and serving in that capacity until 1958. Upon Son Will's retirement in 1952, a Board of Trustees assumed formal control of the school, appointing Follin principal. He later became Director of Alumni and Public Relations at Webb, and died in 1963. The Webb Follin Administration Building and Chapel is named in his honor. The administration had previously been quartered in the Son Will Building.[20]

---

19. See Elizabeth W. Manning, "Manning, John Jr." http://ncpedia.org/biography/manning-john-jr.

20. Holliman, 303. "Webb School History," 1990–1991 catalogue supplement, The Webb School, 2.

Edwin Mims (1872–1959)

Edwin Mims started at Webb School at age 13, graduating in the Class of 1888. He graduated from Vanderbilt University in 1892, took a master's degree there in 1893, and remained at Vanderbilt for another year as a Fellow in English. Mims joined the Trinity College faculty in 1894, taking a leave of absence in 1896–1897 to pursue his doctorate at Cornell University (PhD, 1900). He taught English at Trinity College (now Duke University) and the University of North Carolina until 1912, when he became chair of the English Department at Vanderbilt, a position he held until 1942. From 1928 to 1942, he also chaired the humanities division at the University. He married Clara Puryear of Paducah, Kentucky, in June 1898, and they had four children.

Dr. Mims established his reputation as a leading literary critic in the South with the publication of his biography of Sidney Lanier in 1905. That same year, he became editor of *The South Atlantic Quarterly* at Trinity College. His other books included *The Advancing South* (1926), *Chancellor Kirkland of Vanderbilt* (1940), and *History of Vanderbilt University* (1946). During his long tenure as chairman of the English Department at Vanderbilt, two notable literary movements occurred involving the department: the Fugitive Poets (1914–1925) and the Agrarians (1929–1931). Under Mims, Vanderbilt was probably the first top academic institution in the nation to include creative writing as an integral part of the English Department. Among his many outstanding students were writers Donald Davidson, Robert Penn Warren, Cleanth Brooks, Andrew Lytle, Allen Tate, Merrill Moore, and Jesse Stuart. He was also closely associated through this group of writers with John Crowe Ransom. Dr. Mims served a term as president of the Association of Colleges and Secondary Schools in the Southern States (now Southern Association of Colleges and Schools), as did his mentor, John Webb, and John's nephew, William Alexander Webb '85. A vital force in Southern education for over six decades, Dr. Edwin Mims died in 1959, and was buried in Woodlawn Memorial Park, Nashville. A dormitory, Mims Hall, is named for him at Vanderbilt University.[1]

1. J. Isaac Copeland, "Mims, Edwin," *Dictionary of North Carolina Biography*, Vol. 4, 1991, 280–281. "Edwin Mims" by Kara Furlong, Vanderbilt View–Looking Back: http://sitemason.vanderbilt.edu/vanderbiltview/articles/2011/01/01/looking-back.129111.

CHAPTER SEVEN

SUCCESS AND CONCERNS

If Henry Adams is correct that "a teacher affects eternity; he can never tell where his influence stops," then the Brothers Webb were unqualified successes in the field of secondary or preparatory education. From a rocky start in a moldy church basement in Culleoka, to the exciting "golden period" of Webb School in Bell Buckle in the early 20th century, Sawney and John must have beamed with pride and not a little gratitude as many of their former charges went out to live large lives and, indeed, to take a hand in the game.[1]

The "heyday" of Webb School under the Brothers Webb was probably about 1904 to 1930, when more Webb alumni received Rhodes Scholarships to Oxford University than from any other American preparatory school to that time. Eight former students taught by Sawney and John

---

1. *The Education of Henry Adams*, privately published in 1907, and winner of the Pulitzer Prize in 1919.

Sawney Webb (left) and John Webb in Bell Buckle in the 1890s.

became Rhodes Scholars, a ninth Rhodes Scholar being added before Sawney died. Horace Taft, founder of Connecticut's Taft School, remarked that Sawney Webb—again, John is omitted—"accomplished amazing results with such little equipment that he shames the rest of us."[2]

Webb alumni performed well at Ivy League schools such as Harvard, Yale, Princeton, Columbia, and Pennsylvania, and in top-tier Southern colleges and universities like Vanderbilt, Duke, Emory, Sewanee, Washington and Lee, and in the Universities of Virginia, North Carolina, Tennessee, Mississippi, and Texas. Academically, many won membership to Phi Beta Kappa, the oldest academic honorary in America, and Webb School ranked high in the number of alumni listed in Who's Who in America.[3]

Three Old Boys who studied under the Webbs went on to become governors of states. Ingram Macklin Stainback '01 (1883–1961), who went to Princeton and Chicago, became governor of Hawaii. Fielding

2. McMillin, 8–9. Hodgson, "Webb, William Robert (Sawney)," *Dictionary of North Carolina Biography*, Vol. 6, 1996, 151.

3. Phi Beta Kappa was founded in 1776 at the College of William and Mary in Virginia. Marquis *Who's Who in America* was first published in 1899.

Lewis Wright '12 (1895–1956), who studied at the University of Alabama, served as governor of Mississippi. Finally, popular William Prentice Cooper Jr., '13 (1895–1969), of Shelbyville, Tennessee, son of Webb alumnus William Prentice (W.P.) Cooper Sr. (attended 1888–1890), Speaker of the Tennessee House of Representatives, studied at Vanderbilt, Princeton, and Harvard. He was a three-time governor of Tennessee (1939–1945) and U.S. Ambassador to Peru.[4]

At least four Webb alumni of the period became college and university presidents. John J. Tigert '00, Rhodes Scholar, served as president of the University of Florida and as U.S. Commissioner of Education. Raymond Ross Paty '14, a Bell Buckle native, became president of Birmingham-Southern College and the University of Alabama, and served as Chancellor of the University System of Georgia. Paty was also a member of the board of directors of the Tennessee Valley Authority (TVA). Rhodes Scholar John Andrew Rice '08 was the founder and first rector of experimental Black Mountain College in North Carolina; and William Alexander Webb '85, a nephew of the Brothers Webb and a Culleoka student, led Randolph-Macon Woman's College in Lynchburg, Virginia.

Walter Nance '89, a top Webb School and Vanderbilt University scholar, master of the Chinese language, and one of the creators of Soochow University in China, remembered John Webb: "To me he has been for twenty-eight years my greatest teacher. Some teachers were my masters for a term, or a year; he became more my teacher after I went to Vanderbilt than he had been before."[5]

John J. Tigert '00, was the first child born on the Vanderbilt University campus. He was the grandson of Methodist Bishop Holland N. McTyeire who served as president of the Board of Trust at Vanderbilt. While a student at Vanderbilt, Tigert was one of Chancellor James H. Kirkland's "boys," one of the anointed picked for future success. First Rhodes Scholar from Tennessee, he served as U.S. Commissioner of Education (1921–1928), third president of the University of Florida

---

4. Governor Cooper's son, Jim, a Morehead Scholar at the University of North Carolina, became a Rhodes Scholar and also completed the J.D. degree at Harvard Law School. Jim Cooper is a member of the U.S. House of Representatives from Tennessee. See "The Three Governors From Webb School—Each An Individual," *The Webb School, Alumni Bulletin* (Fall 1977), 3–5. "Thirty Receive Bibles in May Ceremony," *The Webb School Magazine* (Fall 1984), 24.

5. Mims, 7.

(1928–1947), and was inducted into the College Football Hall of Fame (1970) as a standout player for the Vanderbilt Commodores.[6]

Norman H. Davis '97, Ambassador at Large during four presidential administrations, was Woodrow Wilson's Undersecretary of State. Sailing home from the League of Nations meeting in 1919, Davis and President Wilson began discussing their preparatory school educations. When Davis inquired about the top students at Princeton University, where Wilson had been president, Wilson replied: "The best prepared students we get come from a small school in Tennessee known to its pupils as Old Sawney's." Norman Davis, of course, already knew the answer, and it was precisely why he asked the question, finally identifying himself as a Webb School graduate. Wilson, of course, had visited Webb School in 1905 while president of Princeton, and had addressed the students. A Vanderbilt graduate immersed in international affairs, Norman Davis also served as chairman of the American Red Cross. In addition to being a U.S. diplomat at the Versailles Conference (Paris Peace Conference) in 1919, he also attended the 1933 Geneva Conference.[7]

Vanderbilt graduate Frank C. Rand '94 became president of the International Shoe Company. He also served as president of the Board of Trust of Vanderbilt University. Rand Dormitory (1925) at Webb School was named for Frank and his brother, Henry Rand '25.

William Frank McCombs '94 managed Woodrow Wilson's presidential campaign and served as chairman of the Democratic National Committee, 1912–1914. He was thrilled to congratulate Wilson on his presidential nomination at a ceremony in Sea Girt, New Jersey, in 1912.

Old Boy Horace Poynter '95 headed the Classical Department at Phillips Academy in Andover, Massachusetts, for forty years. Remembering Old Sawney and his introduction to Webb School, Poynter wrote: "Although years have passed since that hot August day when I first wended my way up the slope and across the old stile and into the big room to hear

---

6. Edwin Mims, *Chancellor Kirkland of Vanderbilt* (Nashville, TN: Vanderbilt University Press, 1940), 264, 337. See The Webb School home page (Prominent Alumni), http://www.thewebbschool.com/the-school/prominent-alumni/index.aspx; The Webb School (Bell Buckle, Tennessee) Wikipedia (Notable Alumni), http://en.wikipedia.org/wiki/Webb_School_(Bell_Buckle,_Tennessee)#Notable_alumni.

7. Elliott, 231. "School Bells at Bell Buckle," *Southern Living* (October 1979), 44; McLean, 44.

the burning words he poured forth, that lashed my soul with inexorable scorn of the mean and low and vile, I have never forgotten them."[8]

Old Girl Mabel Kate Whiteside '95, a Bell Buckle native, headed the Greek Department at Randolph-Macon Woman's College in Lynchburg, Virginia. She founded the Greek Play Tradition at the college. Her cousin, Henry O. Whiteside '29, served as principal of Webb School during the 1960s.[9]

Mabel's sister, Annie Whiteside '06, was Webb School's first female instructor. A beloved teacher, counselor, and friend at Webb School from 1918 to 1933, she also served as Registrar of Randolph-Macon Woman's College, where her sister taught and where William Alexander Webb '85 had been president.

Annie Paschall '90, a favorite day student of John Webb's, was one of the first female students at Webb to actively pursue the scholarly life. Beautiful, talented, and serious, Paschall was an outstanding student at Vanderbilt University (BA, 1894), which she attended on scholarship. She was offered fellowships to Bryn Mawr College in Pennsylvania and Vassar College in New York. Annie Paschall attended Bryn Mawr for a year and was well on her way to a distinguished academic career when she succumbed to typhoid fever in Atlanta in 1895.[10]

Ewin L. Davis '93 served as chairman of the Federal Trade Commission and was a member of the U.S. House of Representatives for the 5th Congressional District of Tennessee.

Vermont C. Royster '31, who wrote the foreword for Laurence McMillin's *The Schoolmaker* (1971), was editor of the *Wall Street Journal*, won two Pulitzer Prizes, and was the recipient of the American Medal of Freedom, the nation's highest civilian award.

Paul W. Sanger '24 became a pioneer in cardiology and thoracic surgery. The heart surgeon founded the Sanger Clinic in Charlotte, North Carolina (now the Sanger Heart and Vascular Institute) with various locations in the Carolinas. Dr. Sanger died in 1968.

Elton Watkins '07 served as a U.S. Congressman from Oregon from 1923–1925.

8. McLean, 49. McMillin, 133.

9. McLean, 35.

10. Mims, 15. Paul K. Conkin, *Gone With the Ivy: A Biography of Vanderbilt University* (Knoxville, TN: The University of Tennessee Press, 1985), 130–131.

Physician Dr. Dugald McLean '04 of Texas, Rhodes Scholar and Sawney's son-in-law, husband of daughter Emma '02, completed a treatise on his own case of tuberculosis just prior to his death in Asheville, North Carolina. Colonel Robert Bingham of Bingham Military School in Asheville was kind to the McLeans there, Bingham being Sawney Webb's old teacher, mentor, and friend. Dugald McLean was buried in the Webb family plot in Hazel Cemetery in Bell Buckle.[11]

The success of the Webb School program inspired Webb Old Boys and others to establish similar quality schools in the region, institutions which became "feeder" schools to Vanderbilt University and elsewhere. Ed T. Price '00, Sawney's son-in-law and husband of Susan '01, opened the Price-Webb School in Lewisburg, Tennessee, a successful venture until a fire and other problems shut it down in 1925. Morgan began during the Culleoka days. Branham & Hughes, Fitzgerald & Clarke, Peoples-Tucker, Massey, Duncan, and Battleground Academy, were all influenced by Webb School.[12]

Sawney Webb's son, Thompson '07, founded The Webb Schools in Claremont, California, in 1922. Sawney's grandson, William R. "Bob" Webb III '37, "a third generation school man," opened Webb School in Knoxville, Tennessee, in 1955. Both institutions have been highly successful.

> My dear Mr. Webb:—
> I am planning to leave Nashville for Bell Buckle at 9:30 next Monday morning, the 27th, and shall hope to remain there until the train which returns to Nashville at 5 oclock in the afternoon.
> I hope these hours will prove suitable to your convenience and I shall look forward to the occasion with the greatest pleasure
>
> Cordially and sincerely yours,
> Woodrow Wilson[13]

11. McMillin, 165, 171.
12. McMillin, 157. Holliman, 299.
13. Letter dated November 22, 1905, from Woodrow Wilson, President of Princeton University, Princeton, New Jersey, "President's Room," to Mr. W. R. Webb, Bell Buckle, Tennessee, The Webb School Archives.

The *Nashville Banner* for Monday evening, November 27, 1905, reported that "Dr. Wilson went to Bell Buckle this morning, where he will deliver an address before Prof. Webb's school to-day, returning to Nashville this evening." While in Bell Buckle, Woodrow Wilson was entertained in John and Lily Webb's home, the occasion being also John's 58th birthday. Wilson, president of Princeton University, had arrived in Nashville Saturday evening and was a guest of Mr. and Mrs. J.R. Wilson of 1012 Fifteenth Avenue, South. He was the guest of honor and the principal speaker at the Princeton alumni banquet held at the Maxwell House on Tuesday, the 28th, and spoke again to the Nashville Teachers' Association at Watkins Hall on Wednesday night. Wilson left for Princeton on Thursday morning in order to arrive in time to greet President Theodore Roosevelt and other distinguished guests who would be attending the annual Army-Navy football game being played that year in Princeton.[14]

On another front, the famed "Princeton System," the University's honor code, owed its beginning to a Webb Old Boy, Charles W. Ottley '89. In a letter to Son Will, dated July 13, 1916, H. G. Murray, Secretary of The Graduate Council of Princeton University, stated:

> I would like to inform you that the introduction of the Honor System at Princeton, introduced by the class of '93, was owing very largely to your school. Cribbing was rife in Princeton in the Fall of '92. Ottley, who had very high principles and ideas, was disgusted by the way the morale of the undergraduate body was being undermined, and spoke of the Honor System at the Bell Buckle School which he had attended. Some of my class became interested and a propaganda for the Honor System was started, with the result it has been in existence at Princeton since February, 1893 and is an assured and established success. I have written a short account of the Honor System to be placed in the archives of the University and have

---

14. See also Arthur S. Link, ed., *The Papers of Woodrow Wilson*, Vol. 16 (Princeton, NJ: Princeton University Press, 1973), 235.

given these facts. It gives me personally great pleasure to acknowledge our indebtedness to you and the Webb School.[15]

Even today, The Webb School Honor Code, which governs the entire school, requires students to sign a statement on each exam paper: "I give my word of honor as a Webb lady or gentlemen that I have neither given nor received help on this examination."[16]

During the teaching years of Sawney and John Webb, and long before student retention rates were actively studied, Webb School always had a sizable turnover in students. Scores of pupils came and went like a revolving door during the era of the Brothers Webb. Students left for many reasons, personal, financial, and family situation being at the top of the list. Many students and parents learned to loathe Sawney Webb, his stern discipline, corporal punishment, and unbending rules; others failed to compete academically, the classical program of chiefly Greek, Latin, and mathematics too demanding for their previously inadequate academic preparation. Student enrollment in Bell Buckle usually ran about two hundred pupils. While John Webb taught the juniors Greek, he alone taught all the seniors in the Senior Room and there were usually only fifteen to thirty of them.

Probably overstating the reality, John Andrew Rice wrote that no applicant was denied admission as the Brothers Webb felt that "Every boy deserves another chance." Thus "the greatest scoundrels and scholars in the South could boast attendance, long or short, at Webb School."[17]

"And with the tragic exception of one race," as former Webb School administrator and teacher Glenn N. Holliman wrote, "the school opened its doors to all creeds and nationalities." Girls were accepted as day students only, thus the number of girls attending at any given time was very low. Girls were not accepted as boarding students until 1973. Native Americans of the Choctaw Tribe were well-represented in Culleoka and later in

---

15. Transcription of letter dated July 13, 1916 (the year John Webb died), from H. G. Murray, Secretary, The Graduate Council of Princeton University, Princeton, New Jersey, to Mr. W. R. Webb Jr., Bell Buckle, Tennessee, regarding Charles W. Ottley '89, Princeton '93, The Webb School Archives. McMillin, 9. It appears that James "Mac" Brodnax '89, Princeton '94, was also instrumental with Ottley in pressing for an honor code at Princeton University.

16. "School Bells at Bell Buckle," *Southern Living* (October 1979): 44.

17. Rice, 200.

Bell Buckle; a Chinese and a Mexican student attended in Culleoka, and the school openly sought to recruit Mexican and other Latino scholars.

The one "tragic exception" was African Americans. The Webb family had been slave owners in North Carolina; after the Civil War, during Reconstruction, and afterward, the Webb families in Tennessee continued to hire African Americans as servants both in Culleoka and in Bell Buckle. Sawney ran a working farm in both locations. Black men were hired from time to time to help work the farm, and black women were hired generally to cook and help with the children. The Webb families operated "within the limits that the patched but unhealed southern society tolerated." According to Glenn Holliman, the first black students enrolled at The Webb School in Bell Buckle in 1975 were five Africans from Gambia who attended on scholarships. Holliman remembers that the first African American student, a female from Huntsville, Alabama, started in 1977. He added, "Sadly, it was after my time (I left in 1981) before black Americans became regular in attendance."[18]

The decade of the 1920s brought growth and change to the school. An alumni association was formally organized in 1920, followed by a "Board of Trustees of Webb School," replacing the moribund old stock company and conserving the school property. Webb alumni finally persuaded Old Sawney to allow modern dormitories to be built, and clapboard and pot-bellied stoves soon gave way to brick and oil furnaces. Lily Webb, among others, abhorred the boarding house system, and had argued for dormitories all along. Named for generous Old Boys, Jackson Dormitory (1921) and Rand Dormitory (1925) were constructed. The Son Will Building and the John Webb Library were not built until 1927, following Sawney Webb's death.[19]

---

18. Holliman, 291. McMillin, 6. Email to author from Glenn N. Holliman of Newport, Pennsylvania, dated November 5, 2013. Thanks also to Dorothy P. Elkins and Susan Coop Howell for researching when the first African American students enrolled at The Webb School-Bell Buckle.

19. Holliman, 300. McMillin, 167. Glenn N. Holliman: "Finally some dormitories with running water, although the outhouse persisted for the Big Room until its demise in 1950..." Email to author dated November 5, 2013.

William Alexander Webb (1867–1919)

William Alexander Webb graduated Phi Beta Kappa from Vanderbilt University in 1891. Following further study at the University of Leipzig (1895–97) and the University of Berlin (1903–04), he joined his uncles as a new teacher beginning his career at Webb School in the early 1890s. Webb married Mary Lee Clary of Bell Buckle in 1899. He later served as vice president of the Association of American Colleges and as president of what became the Southern Association of Colleges and Schools. Webb served as president of Randolph-Macon Woman's College (now Randolph College) in Lynchburg, Virginia, from 1913 until his death in 1919. A building on that campus bears his name. Wofford College in Spartanburg, South Carolina, gave him an honorary LittD degree in 1911. William Alexander Webb died in Nashville in 1919, and was buried in Bell Buckle's Hazel Cemetery.

Sources: Eva Burbank Murphy, "Webb, William Alexander," *Dictionary of North Carolina Biography*, Vol. 6, 1996, 149–150. McMillin, 95.

CHAPTER EIGHT

COMMUNITY NEAR AND FAR

The John Webb family enjoyed traveling during the summer months, particularly in the Southern, Mid-Atlantic, and New England regions of the country. While at a resort in Rhode Island (son Albert was at Yale), John engaged a distinguished Yale professor in a prolonged discussion of French phonetics, literature, philosophy, and theology. Amazed by the depth of John's knowledge in all things French, C.C. Clarke remarked: "I did not know that there were any men left in the world like Mr. Webb. He has had time to learn so much in such a broad way and of so many things. We university specialists cannot do that."[1]

When Albert entered Yale University to study French, proud father John followed the curriculum himself, studying both language, phonet-

---

1. Mims, 12. McMillin, 138.

ics, and literature and availing himself of the best textbooks and commentaries. His French pronunciation was said to be nearly perfect.[2]

In August 1897, the Brothers Webb and their families attended a gathering of alumni, students, and friends of Webb School at the Tennessee Centennial and International Exposition in Nashville. The "Athens of the South" proudly displayed its full-scale replica of the Parthenon in Athens, Greece.[3]

An honorary doctorate, the Doctor of Laws degree (LL.D.), had been conferred on John Maurice Webb in 1895 by the University of Nashville (later the George Peabody College for Teachers, and now a part of Vanderbilt University). Thereafter, he would be addressed formally in academic circles as Dr. John Maurice Webb, LL.D.[4]

That same year, on November 6, 1895, an organizational meeting of the Association of Colleges and Preparatory Schools of the Southern States (now the Southern Association of Colleges and Schools, SACS) was held in Atlanta, Georgia. Its expressed purpose was to improve education in the South. Seven colleges and two preparatory schools, Webb School one of them, became charter members.[5]

Dr. John Maurice Webb, LL.D., served on the executive committee of SACS beginning in 1896–1897, meeting in Knoxville, Tennessee. He was a vice president in 1897–1898 (meeting in Athens, Georgia), again on the executive committee in 1898–1899 (Columbia, South Carolina), and served as president, the first secondary school official elected president, from 1899–1900 (Charlottesville, Virginia).

John's only known publication, "School Libraries," was published as part of the "Proceedings of the Sixth Meeting" held in Charlottesville from November 1–2, 1900. The association met in Academic Hall on the University of Virginia campus (where John had originally wanted to study after Bingham School) on Thursday evening, November 1. There, John delivered his official address as president.

His "Suggestions For Beginning A School Library," outlining a suitable beginning secondary school library collection, was arranged in four

---

2. McMillin, 135.

3. See Christine Kreyling et al, *Classical Nashville: Athens of the South* (Nashville, TN: Vanderbilt University Press, 1996).

4. McMillin, 136.

5. McMillin, 137.

groups totaling 278 volumes and costing about $305. It was widely distributed. "In preparing this list," John wrote, "I have had before me the needs of Southern schools, especially in rural districts, where there is a dearth of libraries, public and private." He added: "The problem is to put into the hands of the susceptible, but untrained, youth a book that will awaken and direct a latent literary taste, hasten the emotions and form character, leading at last to a taste for the world's best literature." This was originally delivered by John Webb in 1899 at the fifth meeting in Columbia, South Carolina, but was ordered published with the proceedings of the Charlottesville meeting in 1900, where John served as president (See Appendix A).[6]

John again served on the SACS executive committee in 1901–1902 (Oxford, Mississippi), 1902–1903 (Durham, North Carolina), 1903–1904 (New Orleans, Louisiana), and 1904–1905 (Nashville, Tennessee), serving that year on the committee with his protégé, Edwin Mims of Trinity College. John then left the committee, Mims carrying on in his stead.[7]

As SACS continued to grow adding hundreds, then thousands, of colleges and universities and secondary schools, both public and private, the organization became much too unwieldy and demanding for both John and Sawney. The brothers detested the coming Carnegie Unit system of national education which based academic achievement on the number of hours a student spent in the classroom. Webb School was later placed on probation by SACS until the school conformed to the new standard, something which did not take place in John and Sawney's lifetimes, but which was finally realized under Son Will's leadership.[8]

Disillusioned with the proceedings of SACS, John Webb's interest shifted to the highly controversial religious issues of fundamentalism versus modernism or liberal Christianity, and to the scientific (evolution)

---

6. McMillian, 137. *Proceedings of the Sixth Meeting, Association of Colleges and Preparatory Schools of the Southern States* (South Nashville, TN: Publishing House of the Methodist Episcopal Church, 1912), 125–126. "School Libraries" was originally delivered by John Webb in Columbia, South Carolina, as part of the fifth meeting and was included in those proceedings. See "A Short History of the Southern Association of Colleges and Secondary Schools," by Guy E. Snavely, Executive Director, Association of American Colleges, Durham, NC, 1945, 23.

7. See *Proceedings of the Annual Meetings, Association of Colleges and Preparatory Schools of the Southern States, 1895–1911* (Nashville, TN: The Association, 1912). John Webb participated from 1896–1905.

8. Mims, 18. McMillin, 139.

versus Biblical interpretation of creation (creationism). As always, John approached the subject "in the spirit of rational thought" and immersed himself in all aspects of the issue, becoming a knowledgeable and appreciated speaker on the subject both in Bell Buckle, Nashville, and beyond.[9]

John's literary interests led him to start an informal club which met weekly in the superb library of his Bell Buckle home, and which would continue for some twenty-five years. Known simply as "The Club," sometimes as the Dante Club, John's original purpose for the gathering was to encourage his children, nieces and nephews, and others to read good literature; however, as its popularity spread, adults from both town and gown began participating, the venture becoming an object lesson in early adult education. The news spread to Nashville, as well, and John was only too happy to accept the invitation of several clubs in the Tennessee capitol to discuss Dante's works and other fine literature. He regularly met with the Greek Club at Vanderbilt, a club composed mainly of professors, including Chancellor James Kirkland, and a few of the best secondary teachers in the area. John was instrumental in building up the Centennial Club in Nashville, suggested its motto, "Follow the Gleam," and became its guiding spirit, providing the women of Nashville with delightful evenings interpreting Dante's The Divine Comedy and other works. Then there were the Query Club in Nashville, a Dante class in Murfreesboro, and a Book Club in Shelbyville, among others.

When John Webb died in 1916, there was a bust of Dante on the mantel of his study and a gold watch on his desk, appreciative gifts from the ladies of the Centennial Club. The president of the club also represented the Centennial Club at John's funeral.[10]

During the winter of 1912, John taught a Dante class in Murfressboro, Tennessee. Writing to Edwin Mims on February 22, 1912, John offered: "My work in Virgil has not been very successful this year. Dante was a hit. I am called to Murfreesboro this winter to give a course in Dante. I go every Saturday night. Last time I had forty—out when the

---

9. Mims, 19.

10. "John. M. Webb, Noted Educator, Answers Call," *The Nashville Tennessean and The Nashville American*, Thursday morning, April 6, 1916. Mims, 11, 22–23. McMillin, 135–136. "V.U. Chancellor Pays Tribute to John M. Webb," *The Nashville Tennessean and The Nashville American*, Saturday morning, April 8, 1916.

thermometer was 15 [degrees] and snowing. We have ordered 35 texts and about $20 worth of criticism…"[11]

John Webb was also a charter member and onetime president of the Tennessee Philological Association. Founded in 1905, it is now an academic association devoted to the study of language and literature in English and in other languages.

Children were naturally and instinctively drawn to John. They flocked to him whenever he was around, and his charm and wit held their attention "as if by magic." "And none ever failed to receive his cheerful, lovable greetings, whenever he met them—on the street, at play in their yards, or his own home. The light of his eyes and spirit was ever shining upon them." Whenever John traveled, he loved to send postcards home to his young friends. The postcards were a teaching tool, but they also helped to solidify his and their lasting friendships. Once, when a throbbing mastoid necessitated an emergency operation in New York, John, waiting in Union Station in Nashville for the northbound train, requested postcards so that he could send them home to his young friends.[12]

John loved to guide the children in their reading whenever possible, loaning books to families that had none, and always steering their reading habits towards good literature.

John and Edwin Mims enjoyed attending the Chautauqua Lake Sunday School Assembly (now Chautauqua Institute), a summer educational program in southwest New York State. Chautauqua was an experiment in early adult education—vacation learning—that became a national forum for public issues, international relations, science, literature, and the arts.[13]

Much closer to home, their families patronized the Monteagle Sunday School Assembly in Monteagle, Tennessee, near Sewanee and The University of the South on the Cumberland Plateau (Monteagle Mountain). Known as the "Chautauqua of the South," the Monteagle Assembly was unique in that it was ecumenical from its beginning in 1882, though mostly Baptists and Methodists comprised its earliest membership. Even

---

11. John Webb, Bell Buckle, to Edwin Mims, February 22, 1912, Edwin Mims Papers, Vanderbilt University, Nashville, Tennessee.

12. Mims, 23–24. McMillin, 138. Another time, while waiting for the train in Cincinnati, Ohio, with his suitcase at his feet, a man ran by, seized his suitcase, and fled. John Webb returned home with no luggage.

13. Mims, 4, 23. Chautauqua Institution. http://www.ciweb.org/

today, many fifth-generation families traditionally attend the Monteagle Assembly each summer, a Chautauqua still popular with Southerners.[14]

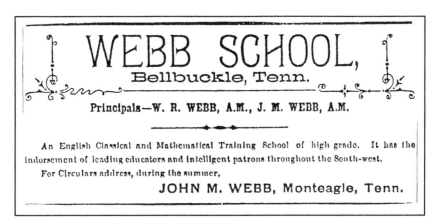

Advertisement for Webb School placed by John Webb while vacationing at Monteagle Sunday School Assembly in Monteagle, Tennessee.

14. Monteagle Sunday School Assembly. http://monteaglesundayschoolassembly.org/; Monteagle Sunday School Assembly, Wikipedia. http://en.wikipedia.org/wiki/Monteagle_Sunday_School_Assembly. See also *Mountain Voices: The Centennial History of Monteagle Sunday School Assembly*, Frank C. Waldrop, editor, printed by The Parthenon Press, Nashville, TN, 1982.

CHAPTER NINE

ELYSIAN FIELDS

The gentle scholar stood in the doorway of the Senior Room, his voice barely audible among the trees. "Books," he said. Nevertheless, the seniors scrambled to their feet and hurried to Old Johnny, toting their split-bottom chairs with them. Other times, John would simply sit inside his $400 classroom-library domain, his own split-bottom chair tilted, and whisper, "Books." Again, the seniors arrived promptly, as if on command. They arranged their chairs "in a circle with imitative tilt," thankful for the open windows and doors in good weather and the pot-bellied stove in poor.[1]

John always began class by asking a simple question, one designed to elicit a broad response from his students, a question that got them thinking in a concentrated way. Every senior knew to have their lessons prepared on a daily basis; to be unprepared would disappoint Old Johnny,

1. Rice, 213.

something no senior ever wanted—the embarrassment and shame would be too much. "It would just break your heart to have Mr. Webb disappointed in you," one senior remembered. "I'd rather have a whipping from Old Sawney than have Mr. John laugh at me," offered another. They had "survived" Sawney Webb and the other teachers of the lower classes. Now they were lofty seniors, and they had earned the right to enter "the sanctuary of the scholar."[2]

John Webb was prone to talking to himself almost anywhere, including in class. Usually it concerned something he had been reading or figuring, something that caught his intense interest. Some thought that John had "gone off his head." John Andrew Rice felt that "the wise are sometimes called mad in a world of fools. The ancients were more discerning. They called them blessed."[3]

Businessman Randolph Elliott of San Francisco, a supposed Webb Old Boy who attended the Bell Buckle school early on, published an article entitled "Old Sawney's" in the August 1920 issue of *The Atlantic Monthly*. This was some of the earliest national print about the Brothers Webb and their school.

In his article, Elliott describes the Big Room and the Senior Room of his day. The Junior Room is not mentioned. Regarding his remembrance of the Big Room:

> It was a large building of pine, with a huge cast-iron stove in the middle. The benches were originally of unplaned oak boards, and the splinters must have presented many points of irritating contact to the first generation of pupils. By the time my brothers and I arrived—years later—they had been worn to a shining glassiness, the smooth surface marred only by knife-cut initials.

The "Senior Hall" (Room) had no benches and at the back of the room was the "small but well-stocked library." When a pupil reached senior status, he was required to go into town and purchase a split-bottom chair for about fifty cents. The chair "traveled with him during school-hours as unfailingly as its shell accompanies the turtle. He took it to

2. McMillin, 130–131.

3. Rice, 214–215.

Latin class, and thence, if he had a free period, to the shade of a tree in the bare, boy-scarred grounds."[4]

The four-year course of study in Elliott's day consisted solely of Greek, Latin, Mathematics, "some English," and one modern language. As seniors they "entered the Elysian Fields of Johnny's classes, for he and he alone taught the seniors." With the solid foundation lain earlier by Sawney Webb and the other teachers of the lower classes, the dead languages of the Classics came alive under John's tutelage, and "we actually read Latin and Greek more easily by far than the average college student reads French and German." Commenting on the national trend of banishing Latin and Greek from American colleges and universities, Elliott offered, "…if you had ever wandered over the Aegean Isles with Johnny, you would feel that in parting with Ulysses you were losing a dear and cherished friend."[5]

Noting at the close of his article that Sawney Webb was no longer in active management of Webb School, his son now in daily charge, Randolph Elliott believed that without Sawney's "morning talk," "it would be for us oldsters as savorless as bread without salt. And Johnny, the every-inch-a-scholar, the giver of life to dead tongues, Johnny has gone—perhaps 'to see the great Achilles whom he knew.'"[6]

Finally, Edwin Mims offered regarding John Webb and the Senior Room: "He was an interpreter for those who were beginning their journey along the road of life. The plain one-room school building was his medium of communication."[7]

---

4. Elliott, 232. It was revealed some years later that the article was actually written by Ida A. Elliott, wife of Eddie Elliott, one of four brothers from Murfreesboro, Tennessee, who attended Webb School and then went on to Princeton University. Eddie Elliott later served as a dean at Princeton. No Randolph Elliott attended Webb School. See "The Webb School and Bell Buckle" by John W. Childress '98, The Webb School Archives.

5. Elliott, 235–236.

6. Elliott, 236.

7. Mims, 14.

CHAPTER TEN

"ENOUGH TO MAKE
THE ANGELS WEEP"

Following completion of his Rhodes Scholarship at Oxford where he studied jurisprudence and with World War I just beginning, John Andrew Rice '08 returned to teach at Webb School for two years (1914–1916) before leaving again to pursue a doctorate in classics at the University of Chicago. Rice and his new bride, Nell Aydelotte Rice, lived in the A.W. Muse house west of the railroad tracks in Bell Buckle.[1]

Nell, the sister of Rhodes Scholar Frank Aydelotte, American secretary to the Rhodes Trust at Oxford and later president of Swarthmore

---

1. Rice, 218–219. Reynolds, 40–43. This home, built circa 1880, is better known locally as the William H. Bomar house. While the Rices lived there, a boarder contracted smallpox and the house was quarantined. Food was delivered to the front porch, the dishes being picked up later after sterilization. The home is across the road from the Paty house and buildings of the defunct Science Hill Academy (Bedford College), ½ mile west of the railroad. See *Doors to the Past: Homes of Shelbyville and Bedford County*, Bedford County Historical Society (Shelbyville, TN: *The Shelbyville Times-Gazette*, 1969), 65.

John Andrew Rice and his Caesar class at Webb School, 1914–1915

College in Pennsylvania, proved quite popular with both Webb faculty and students and with the locals in Bell Buckle. Her gentle Quaker ways charmed everyone who came into her presence. While in Bell Buckle, Nell gave birth to John Andrew Rice II in 1916, the year John Webb died, but the baby lived only a few days into infancy.[2]

John Andrew had come to Webb School in 1905, after his new stepmother had convinced her husband to send the sixteen year-old to Bell Buckle to study with Sawney and John Webb. She had known and befriended the brothers while teaching in Tennessee. "When she talked of Sawney she was like someone who has just come from seeing an exciting play, but when she spoke John Webb's name, her voice changed and her eyes changed, and her words became vague and incoherent, which was a strange thing in her, who could always say what she meant," remembered John Andrew. Joining 150 other boys (and a few girls), John Andrew started as a junior at Webb School and found there the teacher he would revere all his life—John Webb, the gentle scholar.[3]

John Andrew was one of thirty seniors who left Webb School in 1908. He entered Tulane University in New Orleans, where he hoped to find "another John Webb, some professor who would tilt his chair and make a little circle of light." Though disappointed with the formal education he

2. Reynolds, 38–43.

3. Rice, 200. Reynolds, 22–23, 26.

received at Tulane, Rice was selected a Rhodes Scholar from Louisiana in 1911, in part due to a recommendation from John Webb.[4]

Interestingly, John Andrew initially found admission to Tulane University difficult. "Tulane was my first introduction to numerology in education. In Webb School there had never been a hint that accomplishment could be measured by the clock; how many hours and minutes one spent in preparation or recitation was not in question; the question was, "Do you know? In Tulane the question was, "Do you sit, and, if so, how long?" The registrar at Tulane informed Rice that he needed fifteen units (Carnegie Units) for admission, thus John Andrew wrote to John Webb for rescue. "Within a few days it came back all neatly filled out, so many units of this, so many of that, adding up to exactly fifteen units—loving perjury." John Webb had creatively reconstituted into units John Andrew's preparation in Latin, Greek, mathematics, German and English.[5]

A controversial life-long critic of the American higher education system, John Andrew Rice found in his own formal education that only Webb School and Oxford University offered real teaching to elicit real learning.

Mary Emma Harris in her book, *The Arts at Black Mountain College*, wrote about John Andrew Rice, the founder and first rector of the college:

> It was not until he was sent to Webb School in Bell Buckle, Tennessee, that he understood the potential of education to enlighten and prepare one for life. There John Webb, his ideal teacher-philosopher, provided the first and most important role model for the young student, and throughout his life Rice acknowledged his debt and tried to be to others what John Webb had been for him. After leaving Webb School, he attended Tulane University (BA, 1911), an experience that exemplified for him what higher education should not be. Later, as a Rhodes Scholar at Oxford University (1911–1914), he once again experienced a genuine intellectual community,

---

4. Rice, 225. Reynolds, 29, 33.
5. Rice, 225–226. Reynolds, 29–30.

and both Oxford and Webb School were to become models for Black Mountain.[6]

As a Webb School faculty member, John Andrew got to know his "ideal teacher-philosopher" not only as a colleague but as a close friend and confidant. He learned that John was not satisfied with his life; that while he was forever grateful to be able to do what he always wanted to do—to teach—he was also deeply troubled about the growing rift not only between himself and his beloved brother, Sawney, but also between their families.

John Andrew, too, had his own problems. As a teacher at Webb School, he was not popular with Son Will and others. "When he taught here he was excessively lazy," offered Son Will.[7]

The circulars and stationary had always listed both Sawney and John as co-principals of Webb School. Though there was never any formal written agreement, it was understood that the success of their school was due to the unique and very different contributions of both; Sawney, the able speaker, strong disciplinarian and administrator, and a teacher of the lower level students; and John, teacher of Greek to the juniors and mentor to the seniors whom he strove to prepare for college or university and for a satisfying and productive life of the mind. By the end of the first decade of the 20th Century, however, as Sawney's star continued to rise in the public eye—for Sawney "wanted so much to be a great man" and not just "a great teacher"—Old Sawney had grown to view his brother John as "only a teacher" in the school, not an equal in its ownership and administration. The actual running of the school, the bookkeeping, the teaching of the lower classes, the discipline problems both at the school and in the boarding houses, and the often tense interviews with parents, had all fallen on Sawney's shoulders. John was free to teach the school's best students in the Senior Room. John took little part in the daily affairs of the school, and he was never any match for his aggressive and domi-

---

6. Mary Emma Harris, *The Arts at Black Mountain College* (Cambridge, MA: MIT Press, 1987), 8, 303–304. See also Martin Duberman, *Black Mountain: An Exploration in Community* (New York: E. P. Dutton & Co., Inc., 1972), 22.

7. Son Will's letter to brother Thompson Webb, January 1, 1942, W. R. Webb Jr., Correspondence, The Webb School Archives; Reynolds, 42–44.

neering brother. John was eventually forced to take a subordinate position in the school while Sawney and Son Will assumed full leadership.[8]

Strong-willed Lily Webb, a refined and liberated woman unique for her day—and very different from the usually reserved Emma Webb, who generally stayed out of her husband's business affairs—clashed frequently with an equally defiant Sawney regarding school business and her husband's position in the school. She felt that Sawney had little respect for or even sufficient knowledge of the precious accomplishments of her scholarly husband both in Bell Buckle, Nashville, and beyond. It had been hoped—even assumed—by the John Webb family that Albert would someday become co-principal of Webb School alongside Son Will who, upon his return to teach at Webb in 1897, had already been made a co-principal in 1908. Stewart Mims '97, John and Lily's son-in-law, husband to Mary '99, had hoped to assist Albert in the running of the school. Both men knew that Son Will was unpopular with many of the students as he appeared even harder on them than his father.

Old Sawney neither appreciated Albert's ideas for educational change at the school nor, apparently, saw any reason for including him in the school's future. Stewart Mims, like John, was "only a teacher" at Webb. Obviously, to the John Webb family, it appeared that Sawney was trying to take the school away from John while seeking a monopoly for his own family.

Once when John Andrew came to the gentle scholar with a problem that was troubling him, John remarked: "Don't come to me. I no longer have any voice in running the school." This was confirmed when John died in 1916. John Andrew pointed out: "Sawney claimed that, if there was a partnership, it did not go beyond the life of either; and, as there was no written contract, he secured full ownership of the school to himself and his son, Son Will."[9]

A Phi Beta Kappa graduate of the University of North Carolina, Son Will '91 "had the entire management of the school forced on him" as early as 1897, when he returned to teach at Webb. In September of that year, Sawney stepped on a sharp nail while walking over his farm, incurring a painful foot injury which kept him immobile for several months. Sawney turned to his son, not to his brother, John, to lead the school. But Son

8. Rice, 218–220. McMillin, 139–140.
9. Rice, 218–219. McMillin, 139–140. Reynolds, 44.

Will himself stood in awe of his uncle: "...I have never touched a brain that was as scholarly as his, nor one who knew books better than he."[10]

William Robert Webb Jr., Son Will, was made a full partner beside his father and uncle in 1908. Illness had forced Sawney to take a leave of absence for a few months by 1908, and he again placed Son Will in charge of the school. Sawney turned to his son once more when he was appointed a U.S. Senator in 1912, and left for Washington for five weeks. By 1914, Son Will was very much in charge of Webb School.[11]

Old Johnny probably suffered most in the dispute which shattered relations between his loved ones and went to the heart of the school itself. It deeply troubled John, who viewed the family tear as "...enough to make the angles weep." Knowing that he was no longer welcome at the John Webb house, Sawney stopped going. On more than one occasion, John crossed the street to apologize to Sawney for something Lily had said or done.[12]

The ever-growing rift between the families, unknown to the villagers and beyond and shared only with a very few close Webb School alumni, would not implode until John's untimely death.

John Webb kept up with developments in secondary and post-secondary education, and certain issues both interested and concerned him deeply. When John Spencer Bassett, a liberal-minded professor at Trinity College (later Duke University) was in danger of being ousted from his teaching position, John, troubled by the situation, wrote to Edwin Mims:

> The gravity of the crisis impresses me more and more. Trinity is the only small college in the South where such a fight can be made & if the Board stands firm the fight is won & a glorious victory of far reaching influence. Trinity is the only unmistakably unprovincial, yet pos[i]tively ethical college we have. Should she let Bassett go she drops into line with Emory and localizes herself. I say only; for while Vanderbilt

---

10. Holliman, 297. Mims, 5.

11. Holliman, 298. Reynolds, 42. Although he became a principal in 1908, upon his father's death in 1926, Son Will became sole head of Webb School, serving until his retirement in 1952. He died in 1960, and is buried in the family plot in Hazel Cemetery. Since then, The Webb School has been governed by an independent board of trustees.

12. McMillin, 131, 139–140. Reynolds, 44.

is broad enough there is not an ethical spirit manifesting itself organically, however noble some of the members are.

John identified that "persons who have never patronized Trinity" were attacking Professor Bassett, and Old Johnny longed for a "middle way" between secular and liberal colleges and universities, including "ethical," but "narrow" religious institutions of higher education.[13]

Was Vanderbilt University a religious institution? "To affirm that Vanderbilt Univ. is not & never was a church institution is to say she has worn a masque for thirty years," wrote John to Mims.[14]

Both Sawney and John Webb nurtured a strong disdain for the Carnegie Unit, with academic credit being based upon the number of hours spent in the classroom. This system was promoted by the Southern Association of Colleges and Schools (SACS) and endorsed by Chancellor James H. Kirkland and others at Vanderbilt. John remarked to Mims as early as 1908: "I wish I were 'pope' long enough to put 'standardization' on the index."[15]

John Webb: "When you push by external pressure a fourteen-unit standard into the catalog, how are you going to preserve the quality of the unit? Ten honest units is better than fourteen dubious ones."[16]

John attended a meeting of fifteen top secondary-school educators in Tennessee who met in "private conference" in March 1911. They were there to discuss the pressure being placed upon them by Vanderbilt University to conform to the Carnegie Unit system. Applicants who could present certification of the Carnegie Units were being admitted to Vanderbilt without further examination. John wrote to Mims: "[T]hey all agreed that the morale of the student body [at Vanderbilt] was worse than it ever has been in the history of the institution." While many at the meeting strongly supported Chancellor Kirkland on other issues, "Control," John wrote, "seems to be the dominating motive. I cannot make the fourteen

13. John Webb, Bell Buckle, to Edwin Mims, November 23, 1903, Box 3, Edwin Mims Papers, Vanderbilt University; McMillin, 138.

14. John Webb, Bell Buckle, to Edwin Mims, March 22, 1911, Box 3, Edwin Mims Papers, Vanderbilt University; McMillin, 138.

15. John Webb, Bell Buckle, to Edwin Mims, January 10, 1908, Box 3, Edwin Mims Papers, Vanderbilt University; McMillin, 138.

16. Ibid.

units honestly interpreted & honestly enforced with [out] surrendering quality to quantity. To do so would be to go back on history & say that forty years' work for the real & genuine was a mistake. Whither shall I flee from this tyranny?"[17]

Finally, John confided to his dear friend Mims: "Perhaps I ought not to write so freely, but I am so isolated here that I must have a safety valve & you will not get me into trouble."[18]

Old Johnny, who had become Old Jack by this period, told Mims that "I do not think my classroom work was ever better than it is now. But to feel so may be a sign that the sun is westering."[19]

By 1911, John could report to Mims: "As to the Webb School, it never had so many friends or so broad a base of support."[20]

Unfortunately, towards the end of John's life and teaching, some of his Webb School students formed a "union" against him, placing social pressure on any student who dared do more than the required minimum. Try as he might to break the "union" barrier, John told his son Albert that he found it impossible.[21]

John Andrew Rice, the life-long critic of sham in education who penned the "unkindest words" ever written about Sawney Webb, could say this about John Webb: "…I had known only one teacher, John Webb, whom I was willing to call master, only one whom I did not in some measure despise." However, John Andrew could also pay tribute to the school Old Sawney built and nurtured exclaiming that Webb School "had both order and intellectual backbone…its government was for boys as no school I have seen since."[22]

---

17. John Webb, Bell Buckle, to Edwin Mims, March 22, 1911, Box 3, Edwin Mims Papers, Vanderbilt University; McMillin, 139.

18. John Webb, Bell Buckle, to Edwin Mims, March 15, 1907, Box 3, Edwin Mims Papers, Vanderbilt University; McMillin, 139.

19. Ibid.

20. John Webb, Bell Buckle, to Edwin Mims, March 22, 1911, Box 3, Edwin Mims Papers, Vanderbilt University. Edwin Mims received a long letter from Sawney Webb at Bell Buckle on April 5, 1907, regarding Southern affairs including education, Box 16, Webb Correspondence, Edwin Mims Papers, Vanderbilt University.

21. McMillin, 158.

22. Rice, 205, 323. McMillin, 175. Reynolds, 204.

John Andrew noted: "John Webb never thought he knew enough. Sawney read the daily paper and became a prophet...The actor became well known while the scholar's fame spread slowly."[23]

Finally, commenting on the imminent educator John Dewey's respect for the process of learning, John Andrew Rice remarked: "John Webb and John Dewey are the only men I have known who never questioned the individual's right to be alive. They took that for granted, and began from there."[24]

With America's entrance into World War I and the draft affecting faculty recruiting, Webb School hired its first female teacher, Miss Annie Whiteside. Sister of Mabel and a former teacher at Randolph-Macon College for Women, Whiteside was a Bell Buckle native and Old Girl who had graduated from Webb in 1906. Some four hundred Webb School alumni would eventually serve in the armed forces during the First World War.[25]

---

23. Rice, 218. Reynolds, 44.
24. Rice, 324–325, 331. Reynolds, 143.
25. Holliman, 299.

CHAPTER ELEVEN

"O LOVE THAT WILT NOT LET ME GO"

In the winter of 1916, John Webb was seen stumbling from the railroad tracks and into the weeds southeast of the Bell Buckle passenger depot. He was having a stroke and was incoherent. "Old Johnny" walked to the depot daily to pick up his mail, sometimes twice daily, and to stroll safely along the railroad tracks. But today something was very wrong, and he appeared out of control.

John Andrew Rice, who was walking through Bell Buckle at the time, was summoned and came to John's rescue:

> He took his daily walk along the railroad track—it could be relied upon to be dry footing—and one day when I was going through the village someone called me in a worried voice to the depot platform; something was wrong with Mr. Webb.

Down the track I saw him stumbling into the weeds at the side. When I reached him he tried to speak, but his voice was thick.

The doctor said that he had had a slight stroke and might live for a long time, but that he must give up teaching. Two months later he was dead. I had known he would not live, that he could not live without his teaching. He had once said to me, "I couldn't have done anything else. I believe I would have paid to be allowed to teach."

With his father stricken, Albert began talking with Sawney about Old Jack's stake in the school. "Oh! how I would grieve to have our affairs aired before the public," Sawney told Clary Webb '99, his lawyer son.

I educated my brother when it took all the money and all I could borrow. I made sacrifices for him. I relieved him of all drudgery in school work, the lower classes, the discipline and bookkeeping and the unpleasant interviews, the boarding house controversies. I traveled with him again and again, when he was helpless in mind. I loved him all my life. I do not wish Albert to stir up any controversies about business affairs.[1]

At 11 o'clock on Wednesday morning, April 5, 1916, John Maurice Webb died peacefully at home "after an illness of several months." He was sixty-nine years old.

The Nashville Tennessean and *The Nashville American* for Thursday morning, April 6, carried the news of John's death. His portrait, obituary, and various short remembrances by prominent educators and Webb School alumni appeared in the papers over the next several days. The page nine headline of April 6 read:

---

1. McMillian, 158–159. Rice, 222. The railroad was a double track then with both freight and passenger depots. Neither exists today. The trains have not stopped in Bell Buckle since the 1960s.

> JOHN M. WEBB, NOTED EDUCATOR, ANSWERS CALL
> END COMES AT HOME IN BELL BUCKLE
> AFTER ILLNESS OF SEVERAL MONTHS
> BELOVED ALL OVER STATE
> SHOWED GREAT INTEREST IN VANDERBILT UNIVERSITY
> AND WORK OF CENTENNIAL CLUB.
>
> *CAUSES SORROW HERE*
> *MANY WEBB SCHOOL ALUMNI IN CITY.*

Finally, an additional newspaper article published the next day announced:

> NOTED SCHOLAR PASSES AWAY
> PROF. JOHN M. WEBB OF BELL BUCKLE SCHOOL SUCCUMBS TO
> LONG ILLNESS
> HIGHLY REGARDED
> DEATH OF PROF. WEBB SOURCE OF REGRET HERE.

John's obituary stated:

> He is survived by his widow and the following children: Prof. Albert M. Webb, professor of romance languages at Trinity college; Mrs. Benjamin Key of New York city; Mrs. Stewart L. Mims of New Haven, Conn., and Miss Cornelia Webb of Bell Buckle.

The caption under John's portrait, not printed until Sunday morning, April 9, stated that his death "was the cause of widespread sorrow throughout the state."

The articles referred to John as co-principal of Webb School, the position certainly recognized by the John Webb family and their partisans, but no longer by the Sawney Webb family and their supporters.

As it would again in 1926 for Sawney Webb's funeral, the *Dixie Flyer* made an unscheduled stop in Bell Buckle on Thursday, April 6, bringing mourners from Nashville and beyond. Many of John's Old Boys and Girls were in attendance or sent their condolences to the John Webb family. "A large number of alumni will go down to Bellbuckle [sic], as the Dixie Flyer, which by the special courtesy of President Peyton, of the N.C. & St. L. railway, will stop there at 1:16 in time for the funeral exercises at 2:30."

Vanderbilt University was well-represented by Chancellor James H. Kirkland, Dean Wilbur F. Tillett, and Dr. Edwin Mims, among many others, and the whole of Bell Buckle and Webb School, including the Sawney Webb family, were in attendance. Lily's mother, Mary Gillespie (Mrs. Albert M.) Shipp, also paid her respects.

John's service was held at his home on Thursday afternoon at 2:30, officiated by the Rev. T.R. Curtis with assistance from visiting ministers. It was described as "very simple." The senior class at Webb served as pallbearers with the schoolboys also providing the music. Beautiful floral designs came from friends and admirers in Nashville, the faculty of Vanderbilt University, Webb School alumni in Nashville and beyond, and from the faculty of Trinity College in North Carolina.[2]

The large cortege then made its journey down Maple Street to Main and through the village and south by southwest up the hill to Hazel Cemetery. As John's body was being lowered into the grave, the hundreds of mourners "from the village and from far places" listened as some Webb students sang his favorite hymn, "O Love That Wilt Not Let Me Go."[3] Lyrics from the fourth stanza of the hymn read: "I lay in dust life's glory dead, And from the ground there blossoms red Life that shall endless be. Amen."[4]

At a chapel meeting on the Vanderbilt University campus on Friday, April 7, Chancellor James Kirkland remembered John's funeral and paid tribute to John's contributions not only to the University in helping to fix its academic standards in the early days of its history, but also to the advancement of education and scholarship throughout Tennessee and the South:

2. Photocopies from microfilm provided by the Nashville Public Library, Nashville, Tennessee. Microfilm was also read by the author at the James E. Walker Library at Middle Tennessee State University in Murfreesboro. An abbreviated version of these newspaper articles appeared in *The Shelbyville* (TN) *Times-Gazette* for April 13, 1916, and in other area newspapers.

3. Rice, 222.

4. "O Love That Wilt Not Let Me Go," words by George Matheson, 1882, music by Albert Peace, 1884. Holland N. McTyeire, *Hymn Book of the Methodist Episcopal Church, South* (Nashville, TN: Publishing House of the M. E. Church, South, J.D. Barbee, Agent, 1889).

> There was a notable gathering yesterday on the quiet hillside at Bell Buckle, where friends and students of Mr. John Webb laid his body to rest. The students of Webb School, some two hundred, marched together to the house and then to the cemetery. But that was not the unusual feature. The unusual thing was the number of old students and friends who had gathered together; men from prominent walks of life, friends who fill and have filled very important places in public and in private life in Tennessee. There were present many teachers from all over the state; not only students of Mr. Webb but men in the work of teaching who were not his students but who recognized his pre-eminence in this field. Although we met in sadness, yet it was an hour of triumph, the triumph of character, the triumph of truth, the triumph of intellect, the triumph of personality.

Also, John Webb "was not a man of wealth, but he was a man of great wealth of character."

Regarding his influence in Vanderbilt University, Chancellor Kirkland remarked that John's

> hand has been laid on some of the very best men who have gone from Vanderbilt University, and it is not improper that I should at this hour acknowledge publicly and cheerfully the great influence of that man in fixing the students of Vanderbilt University in the years of her history when she most needed such help.

Paying personal tribute, Kirkland remarked:

> If ever I wanted to see the latest book on the vital questions of life, literature, Biblical studies, on Virgil, Homer, Shakespeare, Browning or Tennyson, I was sure to find that book lying on Mr. Webb's table when I entered his home. He was always talking about the very latest thing. He did not talk about dead issues. Now a man like that contributes very largely to his community.

Finally, in lasting tribute, Vanderbilt's chancellor commented that

> Mr. Webb was a man about whom no one ever had an unkind word to say. He was a man whom every one liked and every one respected: a man who did his work in so quiet a way that you failed to realize how great the work was he was doing. During the years of his work in Tennessee, his influence on the young men of the whole south, on the town of Bell Buckle, on Vanderbilt university, has been most marked. Grateful for his help, we shall cherish his memory as one of the best of men.[5]

Reflecting on John's modesty, John Andrew Rice commented:

> John Webb never wanted to be a great anything, and if anyone had used the word of him in his presence, he would have cringed with shame for the speaker. It was only when he lay in his coffin that we could speak without fear of reproof.[6]

Finally:

> John Webb had a wisdom bump in the middle of his forehead, the size of half a walnut. That was the first thing I noticed about him, and the last, when ten years later I told him good-by. We were many then, we who had gathered to give thanks that he had lived.[7]

"Funerals are sad occasions. John Webb's was not; …all spoke of the wonder of his life."[8]

---

5. "V.U. Chancellor Pays Tribute to John M. Webb/Acknowledges His Great Influence in Fixing Standards of the University," *The Nashville Tennessean* and *The Nashville American*, Saturday morning, April 8, 1916.

6. Rice, 221.

7. Rice, 207.

8. Rice, 222.

John Andrew and Nell left Webb School for good just two months after John's death, heading to the University of Chicago.[9]

The gentle scholar was laid to rest in an unmarked grave to the right of that of his two year-old son, Hazel, namesake of the cemetery. Hazel's grave is marked only by a limestone rectangular outline that is quickly disappearing into the ground. Father and son would later be joined by wife and mother in 1929, buried in an unmarked grave beside her husband.[10]

In time, prominent members of the Sawney Webb Family—Sawney and Emma and Son Will and his wife, Louise—would also be interned in Hazel Cemetery, each with a flat stone around the "Webb" family monument. Sawney is buried near his beloved brother who loved him dearly in return.

The gentle scholar, "Old Johnny," later "Old Jack," was gone.

His obituary appeared in the April 13 issue of *The Shelbyville Times-Gazette*, an abbreviation of the Nashville articles. In an adjoining column in the Shelbyville newspaper regarding coming events and personal comings and goings, this notice appeared: "The Book Club meeting was postponed on account of the death of Prof. John M. Webb."[11]

> "He was a man, take him for all in all.
> [We] shall not look upon his like again."
> —*William Shakespeare (1564–1616), Hamlet, Act i, Sc. 2*

---

9. Reynolds, 45.

10. Son Will provided the vital data regarding John's death to the Bedford County authorities. See Louise Gillespie Lynch, compiler and publisher, *Death Records of Bedford County, Tennessee*, 1984, 224. Being buried in unmarked graves, John, Lily, and Hazel Webb's names do not appear on the listing of grave markers in Hazel Cemetery. See Helen C. and Timothy R. Marsh, compilers, *Cemetery Records of Bedford County, Tennessee, Revised 1985, Shelbyville, Tennessee* (Easley, SC: Southern Historical Press, Inc., 1986), 114–131. However, John and Lily Webb do appear in "Find a Grave" entries for Hazel Cemetery: John M. Webb: http://www.findagrave.com/cgi-bin/fg.cgi?page=gr&GRid=75462932; Lily Shipp Webb: http://www.findagrave.com/cgi-bin/fg.cgi?page=gr&GRid=75055156.

11. "Mr. John M. Webb dies at Bell Buckle," *The Shelbyville Times-Gazette*, April 13, 1916.

CHAPTER TWELVE

A LASTING LEGACY

Following John's funeral, Sawney sent Lily a letter of condolence and a check for reputedly $5,000, a sum he felt appropriate now that the school partnership was dissolved. Lily was incensed, however, viewing Sawney's gesture as an insult to the memory and the accomplishments of the man most responsible for the academic prowess of Webb School.

Lily demanded "justice" for John; Albert threatened legal action in federal court to recover his father's stake in the school, retaining lawyer Walter P. Armstrong '01 of Memphis, a Webb Old Boy who later served as president of the American Bar Association. Sawney turned to his attorney son, Clary Webb '99, to represent him, and a settlement quickly ensued. Neither family wanted to air their dirty laundry in public. The John Webb family was awarded about $15,000, and even Walter Armstrong felt that the sum was fair. Armstrong, who heard the worst that the grieving and bitter Lily could say about Sawney, never felt that the schoolmaker was morally reprehensible; he even considered writing Old Sawney's biography, and talked and wrote often of his "humanity."[1]

The rupture between the two families complete, the John Webb family quickly sold their Maple Street home and other properties and abandoned Webb School and Bell Buckle for good. Lily and Cornelia joined Albert and his family in Durham, North Carolina, moving into their spacious home at 1017 West Trinity Avenue. A professor of romance languages and department chair at Trinity College (later Duke University), Albert's own son, John Maurice II, after his grandfather, would grow up to distinguish himself and the family as a faculty and staff member at The University of the South in Sewanee, Tennessee. Images reveal that John, his son Albert, and Albert's son, John Maurice II, looked very similar in appearance.

Of the John Webb family, Albert, Lily, and Cornelia, who never married, lived out the best of their remaining years in Durham. Albert and Cornelia were buried in the family plot in Section 12, Maplewood Cemetery, in Durham.

On October 1, 1917, Lily donated the remaining bulk of her late husband's private library to Trinity College, a transaction brokered by Albert on behalf of the family. Comprising nearly 4,000 volumes, the books were accessioned by the Trinity College Library from January 7–31, 1918, and encompassed some 2,378 titles, many with multiple volumes.[2]

The Annual Catalogue of Trinity College, 1917-1918 stated: "The library of the late John M. Webb of Bell Buckle, Tennessee, containing several thousand volumes, has been given to the College, and is maintained as a separate collection. The books came in 1917 as a gift from Mrs. Webb in memory of her husband, who was for many years one of the principals of the Webb School in Tennessee."[3]

1. McMillin, 159–160. Reynolds, 44–45.

2. In March 1993, Thomas F. Harkins, Associate Archivist at the Duke University Archives, provided this author with photocopies of the pages from the Trinity College Library accession books containing the John Webb Collection and encompassing accession numbers 48481 through 50859. Harkins also provided photocopies of clippings from the *Durham Morning Herald* and the *Raleigh News & Observer* regarding Professor and Mrs. Albert M. Webb, and the 1929 obituary for Albert's mother, Lily Shipp Webb.

3. *Trinity Chronicle*, October 31, 1917. *Annual Catalogue of Trinity College, 1917–1918*, 48. Nannie M. Tilley, *The Trinity College Historical Society, 1892–1941* (Durham, NC: Duke University

Described as "long rated by those who know as one of the most valuable private collections in the Southern States," the library

> represents the collection of the years that Mr. Webb had been teaching. It contains books on English literature, Latin, Greek, Dante, works on history, science, and philosophy, and many of the text books that have appeared in the last quarter of a century. The books are very valuable in themselves, but they have an even higher sentimental value as coming from a sympathetic and discerning friend of Trinity and father of one of our own most devoted teachers—Prof. Albert M. Webb. The Webb collection is to be kept as a separate library, and rooms in the general library have been set apart for these books. The plan is to make this a model home library where the younger students may come into contact with good books under expert direction and may the more easily acquire the habit of improving reading. Funds must be provided for keeping up this library.[4]

As noted above, the John Webb Collection was to be kept intact in its own funded space in the library as an example of a superb personal library of a cultured Southern gentleman. But in time, the collection was broken up and dispersed throughout the Trinity College collection and now Duke University's library system, cataloged first by the Dewey Decimal system and now the Library of Congress classification system. While it has been conjectured that the John Webb Collection formed the nucleus of the Duke Divinity School Library, this is untrue even though a goodly number of John's books reside on its shelves. One can, as this author has done, go to the Divinity School library stacks to find specific titles listed in the accession books, pull them off, and find John Webb's inscription.[5]

Press), 74 (footnote 35).

4. *Report of the President of Trinity College to the Board of Trustees, June, 1918*, Durham, North Carolina, 4–5.

5. Research visit by author to Duke University, Durham, NC, February 1993. It has been noted that John Webb wrote his name, the date purchased, and the cost in each of his books, but this author found only his name and sometimes the date.

Book plate for the John M. Webb Collection at the Trinity College Library (Duke Divinity School Library, Durham, NC)

The John Webb donation, coupled with other recent acquisitions by the Trinity College Library, were described by Earl Porter in *Trinity and Duke, 1892-1924* as "notable accessions, but they were not supplemented by purchases in sufficient quantity to establish the beginnings of a research library."[6]

Lily's father, Dr. Albert Micajah Shipp, a prominent Methodist minister and church historian, author of *The History of Methodism in South Carolina* (1883), died in 1887, and was buried in the Gillespie Cemetery near Wallace, South Carolina. Inspired by the donation of her husband John's personal library to Trinity College, Lily's sister, Professor Albert

---

6. Earl W. Porter, *Trinity and Duke, 1892–1924: Foundations of Duke University* (Durham, NC: Duke University Press, 1964), 188.

Webb's aunt, Miss Susie V. Shipp, donated some 2,000 volumes of Dr. Shipp's personal library to Trinity College in 1921. This private library of a long-time president of Wofford College in Spartanburg, South Carolina, and later theology professor, seminary dean, and vice-chancellor at Vanderbilt University, was described as "splendidly selected."[7]

---

7. *Trinity Chronicle*, December 14, 1921. *Annual Catalogue of Trinity College, 1921–1922*, 167. Tilley, 74 (footnote 35). While in Paris with his wife during the summer of 1927, Professor Albert Webb was authorized by Duke University to purchase the private library of the distinguished French scholar and critic, Gustave Lanson. This collection added some 11,000 volumes to Duke's library. See Durden, 170. Louise L. Queen, "Shipp, Albert Micajah," *Dictionary of North Carolina Biography*, William S. Powell, ed., Vol. 5 (Chapel Hill, NC: The University of North Carolina Press, 1994), 334. Lily Shipp Webb's mother, Mary Jane (Gillespie) Shipp, lived with her husband, Dr. Albert M. Shipp, at Rose Hill Plantation in Marlboro County, near Wallace, South Carolina.

CHAPTER THIRTEEN

SORROWFUL ANGELS

Lily Webb remained bitter towards Sawney till the end. On December 31, 1917, Sawney wrote to "Sister Lillie" telling her about the sale of "Jungle Farm" and of his depositing the note in the Bank of Bell Buckle. The note, part of Sawney's profit on the real estate deal, was due in 1922, with interest payable annually and endorsed by Sawney. "I sincerely hope it will add to your comfort," he wrote Lily. "It will always be a pleasure to me to serve you. Affectionately, (signed) W.R. Webb"

Lily's rely to "Brother Sawney" stated in part, "I infer that you are offering me a gift, as you say this note represents part of your profit on sale of Jungle farm. Unless I hear from you within 3 days that this note is in settlement of an indebtedness to my husband's estate, I will notify Bank of Bell Buckle to return said note to you. Justice to me is inexpressibly precious, but a gift I cannot accept."

Sawney replied:

> It is difficult to estimate obligations that grow out of a life time of obligations that exist between brothers, who were partners in business. There is no standard of measure in such cases. John assisted me in many ways, as well as financially. I made a good trade in the Jungle farm. I got a good profit. I would have shared it with John if he were here. I would love to share it with those who were nearest to him. He assisted me and made the good trade possible. It will be a pleasure to share this, or other good things with those he loved. I shared with him in his life time…

In the end, Lily had the bank return the note to Sawney stating that while John had assisted Sawney financially in the Jungle farm transaction, he would have never expected repayment.

> …[H]e did not intend to claim, or wish us after his death to claim any return. That was one of those accounts not intended to be settled in this world." Commenting on their "changed relations," Lily pled, "We cried to you for justice—elemental justice. You meted out to us the strictly legal justice that the laws of Tenn[essee] allow for those who lack a written contract, duly signed and sealed—a situation of which we would have scorned to take advantage if you had died first. So we paid the penalty incurred by Mr. John Webb for his confidence in your good faith to keep the verbal contract made in the happy Culleoka days—the beginning of your prosperity and fame—and his dearest plans for me failed. You changed your mind as to his value and his rights after you said to me "John and I are absolutely equal in the ownership of the school." I am in no uncertainty as to his knowledge that he was Joint Founder and Owner of Webb School. But, without that restraining paper the idea of monopoly captured your imagination and you presumed to sit in judgment on the relative values of your work and his, and yours loomed larger because it was more conspicuous. You lacked the insight to discern the influences

of that powerful, quiet spirit that worked silently and continuously like the forces of nature and you said in your heart "It is right that I should have the school—John is nothing but a teacher." Nothing but a teacher!

Margaret [Woodrow] Wilson exclaimed, when here last spring [1917], "I was a child in thought when I first visited you. He [John] waked me up and inspired me with a longing for growth. I had never met such a man. Who can take his place? No other school that I know of ever had a man like him. He was wonderful."[1]

I myself rejoiced often as I saw in the delight of guests that his gifts of mind and graces of spirit made our home a center of light and joy to many. You and Will are in full possession of the school and the financial benefits of his name and fame, the results of his long life as a teacher—"the foremost teacher of his generation in the South" as one has recently written me. Papers duly signed and sealed, the value of which you now appreciate, secure you and yours in the future. Your changed attitude has placed a gulf between us. There was a time when I could even ask favors of you for then in those days I felt my interests were as safe with you as they were in the hands of my husband.

I face declining years with head erect and heart at rest, protected by a band of seven sons and daughters who, one and all

---

1. Margaret Woodrow Wilson (1886–1944), eldest daughter of President Woodrow Wilson and Ellen Louise (Axson) Wilson, served briefly as First Lady of the United States upon her mother's death in 1914, and until President Wilson remarried in 1915. Educated at Goucher College in Baltimore, she trained in voice and piano at Peabody Institute of Music. The soprano debuted with the Chicago Symphony Orchestra in Syracuse, New York, in 1915, and performed at camps and benefits for the American Red Cross during World War I. A professional vocalist, she made several recordings around 1918. Margaret later became enthralled with Indian mysticism and in 1938 went to Pondicherry, India, to visit the Sri Aurobindo Ashram. She ultimately decided to join the ashram, living out the remaining six years of her life as "Nishtha," Sanskrit for "sincerity." She died in 1944 at age 57 of uremia, an illness accompanying kidney failure, and was buried in Pondicherry. See Margaret Woodrow Wilson: http://search.yahoo.com/search;_ylt=AlIZsFvhQMS.ROOKIdCOZRabvZx4?p=Margaret+Woodrow+Wilson&toggle=1&cop=mss&ei=UTF-8&fr=fp-yie8.

rejoice that in their hearts their father lives again. In solemn candor, without bitterness I make my reply.[2]

Harriet Elizabeth Lillie (Shipp) Webb died on Thursday, June 27, 1929, in Durham, North Carolina. *The Raleigh News & Observer* for June 30 included Lily's obituary entitled "Mrs. Lily S. Webb Passes at Durham, Was Widow of The Late J.M. Webb, of Famous Bell Buckle School." The obituary noted: "The deceased was 80 years old, and death had been imminent for some time." Following a 2:30 funeral service at Albert's home on Friday conducted by Dr. W.A. Stanbury and Professor James Cannon III, her body was shipped back to Bell Buckle to be interned next to her husband and near her son in Hazel Cemetery.

Lily's obituary continued: "Surviving are one son, Dr. Albert M. Webb, of Duke University; three daughters, Miss Cornelia Webb, of Durham; Mrs. [Stewart] Mims, of Greenwich, Conn., and Mrs. Ben Witt Key, of New York City; one sister, Miss Susie V. Shipp, of Durham, and three brothers, Judge S.W.G. Shipp, of Florence, S.C., Thornwell T. Shipp, of Chattanooga, Tenn., and Albert M. Shipp, of Nashville, Tenn. Prof. Shipp Sanders, of the University of North Carolina, is a nephew."[3]

Albert Micajah Webb '95 died on September 8, 1965, age 88, at the Duke Medical Center. John and Lily's first child, he was born in Nashville, Tennessee, during the Culleoka years. Albert attended Webb School in Bell Buckle before transferring to Phillips Academy in Andover, Massachusetts, one of the prominent New England preparatory schools. This is the same school Son Will attended. Albert completed his BA degree at Yale University in 1901, and his master's degree there in 1903. He further studied at the Sorbonne in Paris 1907–1908, at the University of Madrid in 1908, and in Florence in 1923. Albert joined the faculty of Trinity College (later Duke University) in Durham,

---

2. Copy of a transcription by Rhodes Scholar Dr. Albert G. Sanders '01 of Jackson, Mississippi, from letters (1917–1918) received from his sister. His uncle by marriage was John Webb. Only Sawney's initial letter in this exchange with Lily is dated in the transcription. These letters were submitted by Sanders to Laurence McMillin for possible use in *The Schoolmaker*. Of Lily Webb's four surviving children, one son and three daughters, the son and two of the daughters married, giving her seven "sons and daughters" in all.

3. *Raleigh News and Observer*, June 30, 1929. Interestingly, Lily (Shipp) Webb's obituary did not appear in either of Durham's newspapers, the *Herald* or the *Sun*. Thanks to Lynn Richardson, Local History Librarian, North Carolina Collection, Durham County Library, for verifying.

North Carolina, in 1903, serving as a professor of romance languages and department chair until his retirement in 1947. He married Clara Louise Jones in 1914, and their son, John Maurice II, after his paternal grandfather, was born the next year.[4]

Two of John and Lily's daughters married classmates at Webb School in Bell Buckle. Mary Gillespie Webb '99 married Stewart Mims '97 and Sarah Webb '01 married Benjamin Key of her class. Cornelia never married.[5] Mary (born October 1881 in Tennessee) died in Greenwich, Connecticut on January 16, 1957; Sarah (born January 6, 1884, in Tennessee) died in New York on September 21, 1963; and Cornelia (born November 29, 1879, in Tennessee) passed in Lynchburg, Virginia, in March 1973. Finally, son Hazel Alexander Webb (born 1886 in Tennessee) died in Nashville, Tennessee, on October 22, 1888.[6]

Albert M. Webb's son and John's grandson and namesake, Dr. John Maurice Webb II, was born May 31, 1915. He received his BA degree from Duke University in 1936, MA from Yale University in 1938, and his PhD from Duke in 1954. John joined the faculty of The University of the South at Sewanee, Tennessee, in 1946, serving successively as professor of history, dean of men, acting dean of the college of arts and sciences, and as associate dean of the college. The Francis S. Houghteling Professor of American History, Dr. Webb served as dean of the college from 1979–1980, retiring in the summer of 1980.[7] In 1992, he was presented the Distinguished Faculty Award by the Associated Alumni, the top honor annually bestowed upon a faculty member at Sewanee.[8]

Dr. Webb did not attend The Webb School but later, as a "friend" of the school, was elected to The Webb School's Board of Trustees in 1963, and served a long tenure. On February 5, 1993, he attended the dedication of the William Bond Library at The Webb School, the modern hi-tech edifice replacing the John Webb Library (1927) named for

4. Obituary, Albert M. Webb, *Durham Morning Herald*, September 9, 1965. Robert F. Durden, *The Launching of Duke University, 1924–1949* (Durham, NC: Duke University Press, 1993), 9, 145.

5. *Alumni Directory, The Webb School, 1984* (Bell Buckle, TN: The Alumni Association of The Webb School, 1984).

6. Ancestry.com. WebbArchives 1870, Webb Family Tree, Family Group Sheet.

7. Data courtesy of Annie Armour, University Archivist, The University of the South Archives, Sewanee, Tennessee, February 28, 2013.

8. *The Webb School Magazine* (April, 1993), 22, The Webb School Archives.

his grandfather. The John Webb Library Award is bestowed annually to a deserving student at graduation.[9]

Dr. John Maurice Webb II died on April 29, 1999, and is buried with his wife, Ellen Farnum Webb, in University Cemetery at The University of the South in Sewanee, Tennessee.[10]

In 1904, Sawney Webb was offered but declined the presidency of the University of Tennessee in Knoxville.[11]

On March 31, 1912, U.S. Senator Robert Love Taylor of Tennessee died. Sawney Webb, by then the "South's greatest teacher of boys," was elected U.S. Senator by the Tennessee state legislature to serve out Taylor's term—one month and a day or five weeks (January 24 to March 3, 1913). During his brief service in Washington, D.C., the reconstructed old Confederate managed to get a bill passed prohibiting desecration of the American flag and gave an impressive speech in support of prohibition to a packed Senate chamber. Sawney also attended Woodrow Wilson's first inauguration. When the *Literary Digest* reported the inauguration, white haired and bearded Old Sawney appeared in the cover photograph.[12]

He served on Bedford County's draft exemption board during World War I. In 1922, he received honorary doctorates from the University of

---

9. *The Webb School Magazine* (April, 1993), 22, The Webb School Archives. See also *Duke University Alumni Directory, 1985* (White Plains, NY: Bernard C. Harris Publishing Co., Inc., 1985). The William Bond Library at The Webb School is named for William West Bond, Class of 1903, who was the architect and designer of the Holiday Inn hotels. Thanks also to Matthew Wilson, Director of Alumni Giving and Alumni Relations, The Webb School, Bell Buckle, Tennessee, for data regarding Dr. John Maurice Webb II, April 18, 2013.

10. Site inspection of Dr. and Mrs. Webb's graves at Sewanee by the author, July 22, 2013.

11. McMillin, 146.

12. McMillin, 154–156. Wills II, "Webb, William R. "Sawney" (1842–1926)," *The Tennessee Encyclopedia of History and Culture*, Tennessee Historical Society (Nashville, TN: Rutledge Hill Press, 1998), 1044. Hodgson, "Webb, William Robert (Sawney)," *Dictionary of North Carolina Biography*, Vol. 6, 151. Senator Taylor was the maternal grandfather of renowned writer and teacher of writing, Peter Taylor, recipient of the Pulitzer Prize for Fiction for *A Summons to Memphis* in 1987. Peter Taylor was buried in University Cemetery at Sewanee, Tennessee, along with fellow writers and old friends, Allen Tate and Andrew Lytle. However, according to Tom Watson of The University of the South Archives, Taylor's wife, the poet Eleanor Ross Taylor, later had his ashes reinterred in a family plot in Virginia.

North Carolina, Chapel Hill, and from Erskine College in Due West, South Carolina.[13]

Webb Follin Sr. '08, a Webb teacher who later became the school's principal, traveled with Sawney in his twilight years. Follin remembered the days before small-town hotels included twin beds in their rooms: "It was like climbing into bed with Moses."[14]

William Robert "Sawney" Webb did not go gently. Before he died in his Maple Street home on Sunday, December 19, 1926, at age 84, he lingered for days caught up in a delirium of dreams about people and places in his past. In one of these dreams he saw his beloved brother, John, living in a beautiful house and standing next to his handsome son, a great artist who had decorated the home. The sight both thrilled and pleased Old Sawney. His children believed that the attractive young man was their cousin, Hazel Alexander, John and Lily's winsome baby boy who lived only a couple of years, and whose name graces Bell Buckle's cemetery.[15]

The Webb Tower, a thirty-foot steel frame with platform, was constructed in 1916 (the year of John's death) in a single day by Webb School alumni on High Windy at Blue Ridge community near Asheville, North Carolina. When Sawney died in 1926, the Webb Tower was discovered broken by former Webb School students. It had been seen intact just the day before Sawney's death. One newspaper account reported that the tower "bowed its head in apparent grief" over Sawney Webb's death.[16]

---

13. Wills II, "William R. "Sawney" Webb," 1044, and Frere, "Webb School," 1043, *The Tennessee Encyclopedia of History & Culture*, Tennessee Historical Society (Nashville, TN: Rutledge Hill Press, 1998). Hodgson, "Webb, William Robert (Sawney), *Dictionary of North Carolina Biography*, Vol. 6, 151. McMillin, 166.

14. McMillin, 169–170.

15. McMillin, 164, 171–174. The Old Salem Cemetery in Bell Buckle is much older than Hazel Cemetery, but is small. It is located a little past Hazel Cemetery going towards Wartrace on Route 269 (Bell Buckle-Wartrace Road), and is located on a small rise on the left.

16. *Asheville* (NC) *Citizen*, January 2, 1927. The article includes the history of Webb Tower. McMillin, 5–6, 173.

Why is John Webb Buried in An Unmarked Grave?

While some have speculated that John Webb was buried in an unmarked grave in Hazel Cemetery to emphasize his "invisibility" to Sawney Webb and his family, such is not the case. John was an intensely humble man who may have viewed grave markers as a sign of vanity before God. His strong religious beliefs allowed him to surrender all to his Lord and to be "known but to God." Hazel, John and Lily's son and the cemetery's namesake, was first buried in an unmarked grave in 1888, save for a limestone rectangular outline. When Lily died in 1929, she too was interned next to John in an unmarked grave.

CHAPTER FOURTEEN

RETURN TO CULLEOKA AND BELL BUCKLE

Culleoka

A visit to Culleoka, Tennessee, an unincorporated community in Maury County some ten miles from Columbia, the county seat, reveals little evidence that the Brothers Webb were ever there (1870–1886). The Culleoka Academy is no longer, and the modern Culleoka School (K–12) now occupies the site. Before expansion of that complex, the site of the imposing wooden Culleoka Academy building with its "dubious steeple" was pointed out about where the ball field was. Its location was pinpointed from a Sanborn fire insurance map of the village.

In January 1989, the author visited Culleoka for the first time. My guide was Betty Gibson, a former postmaster of Culleoka and local historian-genealogist, and her husband, Leonard, a World War II veteran. We toured the Methodist Church, including the basement where the

Culleoka Institute was located, and then found the site of the Culleoka Academy building on the playing fields behind the present public school. We ventured around the village including walking across the trestle over Fountain Creek.

The site of Sawney Webb's farm is unrecognizable. Next to the railroad track looking south of Culleoka, the farmhouse was to the right of the track at the top of a hill, and the venerable Batch, housing for students of limited means, was located to the left of the track opposite the farmhouse. The house and barn are gone, as is the Batch, and the site is overgrown with woods and underbrush. The road across meandering Fountain Creek, with its quaint little bridge, winds up the hill to parallel the railroad track just behind the site of the Sawney Webb farm. After Sawney sold the property and vacated Culleoka, the house burned, and some section houses for the railroad were later built on the property which, in turn, also burned. It is evident that other uses have been made of the property which is today densely overgrown and non-descript.

The Methodist Church circa 1867, where the Culleoka Institute (later Culleoka Academy) was originally founded in the basement and where Sawney Webb came to teach in 1870, survives though little of the congregation remains and the building appears to receive only minimal use today. Signage on the church building denotes its place on the National Register of Historic Places and with the Tennessee Historical Commission. But there is no mention of the school and the contributions of Sawney and John Webb or the other teachers who both preceded and followed them. In fact, there is no signage at all in Culleoka informing the visitor that the so-called "original" Webb School was founded there. But given the circumstances surrounding the Webb Brothers' move to Bell Buckle, perhaps that is understandable.

There are two entrances, back and side, to the basement school of the church. The sanctuary upstairs was utilized by the school for lectures, debates, and for commencement. The inside steps leading down from the chapel are modern.

An ancient oak tree, said to be one of the oldest in Middle Tennessee, stands to the left of the Methodist Church, and a remodeled former log house, reported to have housed students, stands on the right. The Masonic Lodge, downhill to the rear of the church, is one of the oldest buildings in Culleoka, as is the old but current post office in what is left of the business block.

By John Webb's own count, his and Lily's home was exactly forty-five yards downhill from the Methodist Church, which may have placed it along the main road that abruptly turns left past the business block. It has yet to be determined if the John Webb house is still standing—there may be a couple of possibilities—but additional research, including a deed search of those properties, would need to be made. Two homes, both painted white and just across the main road, seem likely candidates. John's original classroom, separate from the church basement school and next to a saloon, burned with the saloon when it and other stores in the business block burned.[1]

Reportedly, there was a large boulder or boulders in the yard of the John Webb home where the children played, and at least one image of John with some of his students (in The Webb School Archives) appears to bear this out.

Thus, other than the Methodist Church where Sawney Webb came to teach in its basement in 1870, there is little for the visitor to see in sleepy little Culleoka regarding the Webbs. Even The Webb School family appears to have taken little interest in their Culleoka beginnings.

Bell Buckle

In the Middle Tennessee county of Bedford, home of the Tennessee Walking Horse ("The Celebration") in the county seat of Shelbyville, locations with names like Bell Buckle, Wartrace, Normandy, Bugscuffle, and Tenpenny Hill are intriguing. Turning right off U.S. Highway 231 a few miles north of Shelbyville onto the "Sawney Webb Memorial Highway" (State Highway 82), the two-lane road meanders through beautiful countryside dotted with horse farms and upscale dwellings of commuters to Shelbyville, Tullahoma, Murfreesboro, and Nashville, and perhaps even Chattanooga. Coming up Science Hill into Bell Buckle, still one half mile west of the railroad, one passes the site of the old Bedford College on the right beside the Paty house, and the William H. Bomar

---

1. McMillin, 88–89. Several sources report that the Methodist Church was not built until 1868. Letter from the author to a Mr. Scruggs, store-owner in Bell Buckle, Tennessee, January 7, 1989, copy sent to then Headmaster Jackson E. Heffner at The Webb School, Bell Buckle.

brick house (formerly the A.W. Muse residence circa 1880) on the left where John Andrew Rice and his new bride lived for a couple of years. The road proceeds downhill across Bell Buckle Creek, from which the town derived its name, and over the railroad track past the business block and residential area before reaching The Webb School on the eastern edge of town. Main Street is now called Webb Road, East and West.[2]

Bell Buckle's population has remained around 400 for decades. The population of Bell Buckle was 391 in 2000, but the town is beginning to experience yet another "boomlet." Today it is more than 450 people.[3]

The trains have not stopped in Bell Buckle since the 1960s. Now a single track, the former double track with both passenger and freight depots are gone. The site of the passenger depot is near the present Bell Buckle Post Office which, in turn, is near the old Lynch House Hotel—the railroad hotel—that temporarily housed many Webb School students when they first arrived and their parents and families when they visited. Today the hotel is a private residence. The spring where the cow bell and buckle were allegedly found tacked to a tree and provided the town with its unique name is reportedly just south of the former hotel at the foot of Hinkle Hill.

The remaining business block includes the Bell Buckle Café, where the post office was located. The former H.E. Dean's Drug Store had a soda fountain, once a local favorite. William P. Crawford's General Merchandise Store later became the popular Phillips General Store. The Bank of Bell Buckle was once housed in what is now Hilltop Antiques. The bank's vault with small wall safe is a popular curiosity for Hilltop's customers. The site of the People's Bank is now part of the old hotel property.

On the site of the passenger depot today sits a restored early 20th-century caboose, a reminder of Bell Buckle's past as a railroad town.

Home to Margaret "Maggi" (Britton) Vaughn, Poet Laureate of Tennessee; noted sculptor Russ Faxon; and at one time a museum for Grand Ole Opry stars Charlie and Ira Louvin—the Louvin Brothers—Bell Buckle hosts three very popular events each year for the general public:

---

2. Salem Academy was founded in 1820 as the area's first school. It later morphed into Science Hill Academy, and still later Bedford College, a non-descript educational entity. The Bell Buckle public school was built in the 1920s.

3. Current population figure courtesy of Bell Buckle's Chief of Police, Tommy L. Wiley, April, 18, 2013.

The Webb School Arts and Crafts Fair in October; the RC Cola & Moon Pie Festival in June; and the Annual Bike Rally and Poker Run Festival in August. A member of Tennessee Backroads, Bell Buckle is also the smallest Tree City USA town in Tennessee.[4]

The "Bell Buckle Historic District" was placed on the National Register of Historic Places in 1976, including the Junior Room and the Son Will Building at The Webb School.

Neither of the Maple Street homes of John and Sawney Webb stand today. A modern home sits on the site of John Webb's house, and the lot where Sawney's house stood—still the property of The Webb School—is empty, utilized mainly for special occasions, including the annual Webb School Arts and Crafts Fair. The gate posts to the property were removed to the entrance of the walkway leading up to the steps of the Webb Follin Administration Building and Chapel at The Webb School. The state historical marker for Webb School has been moved there as well. Sawney's barn, the design of which was reminiscent of that of the Senior and Junior Rooms, burned in 2006.

The Bell Buckle United Methodist Church on Maple Street, the former Methodist Episcopal (M.E.) Church, South, the Webb brother's church, has been renovated and enlarged and continues to bring the Gospel to the community and The Webb School.

A front door (with colored glass border) of a small residence on Abernathy Street is reportedly all that remains of the John Webb house. It was supposedly a side door to the house.

The Webb School has changed considerably over the years and features a top-notch campus and physical plant that are the envy of its competition. Signage on several campus buildings repeat some of Sawney's notable sayings, and the side of a girls' dormitory building features a large listing of Webb's ten Rhodes Scholars, adding number eleven and leaving it blank with a question mark.

The Junior Room, now used again as a classroom, is the only remaining structure of the original Bell Buckle campus.

---

4. A former working drummer, the author backed up Charlie Louvin one night at a club in McMinnville, Tennessee. The Louvin Brothers were originally from Alabama. The Louvin Brothers Museum is now located in the Smoke House Restaurant and Trading Post in Monteagle, Tennessee.

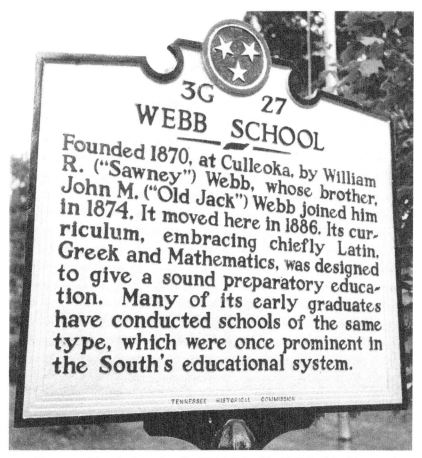

Tennessee historical marker for Webb School in Bell Buckle. The text is mistaken, as John Webb joined his brother, Sawney, in January 1873.

Leaving Bell Buckle going south by southwest on County Highway 269 (Bell Buckle-Wartrace Road) towards Wartrace, leads one up the hill to Hazel Cemetery on the right. Here John, Lily, and Hazel Webb, the cemetery's namesake, are buried beside each other in unmarked graves. They are located near the marked graves of the Sawney Webb family around the "Webb" family monument.

EPILOGUE

R hodes Scholar William Yandell Elliott '13 offers a unique take on the Brothers Webb; perhaps a partisan of Old Johnny, he certainly recognized the myriad contributions of Old Sawney.

Remembering, as many felt, that a visit to the John Webb home could almost be an event in one's life, Dr. Elliott recalled: "The memorable evenings that we used to spend with him reading the New Testament in Greek and absorbing the quiet peace of his home, being initiated into Dante and learning that there were mysteries of Sanskrit too holy for our young reach—those were the things that planted the seeds of beauty and grew the roots that put down into the deep soil of classic humanism for Webb students." He added: "John Webb open[ed] up a new world and new dimensions for all the possible worlds in which we were later to live. His humility of spirit served to reveal the greatness of the man. He commanded both respect and love."[1]

1. Mims, 8.

EPILOGUE

William Y. Elliott graduated from Vanderbilt University in 1917, completed a certificate at the Sorbonne in Paris in 1919, and took the D.Phil degree at Balliol College, Oxford, in 1923. Elliott's son Ward, a professor of government at Claremont McKenna College in California, remembered: "My father was a classics major at Vanderbilt, no doubt owing to the Webbs' influence, and he read PPE [Philosophy, Politics, and Economics] at Oxford, which is what people who would have read classics in the 19th century did in the 20th." Long associated with Harvard University, Dr. Elliott chaired the department of government, served as an eminent professor of history and government, and directed the Harvard Summer School. Among his many outstanding students at Harvard, Dr. Elliott mentored future Secretary of State Henry Kissinger. William Y. Elliott served as a political advisor to six U.S. presidents.

In his address to the graduating Class of 1960 at Webb School in Bell Buckle, Dr. Elliott first expressed his concern that Webb School had dropped Greek from its curriculum while continuing with the Latin. "A curriculum of the classical studies is the best tested education," he proffered. He added: "I can say that Webb men were among the few as Rhodes Scholars whom the British at Oxford rated high in the examinations for honors schools because of their knowledge of Greek and Latin."

Recalling the examples set by his schoolmasters at Webb, Elliott offered: "But, it was by the example of Old Johnny, that great scholar of Greek, Sanskrit, and Dante, that we learned what a great scholar was. And from Old Sawney, the old soldier, the Senator, that we learned what was a stern but just man. Old Sawney birched us into Latinity but Johnny loved and wept us into Greek, showing a greater rebuke by his disappointment in us that any whipping Sawney ever gave."[2]

Dean Wilbur F. Tillett of Vanderbilt University, whom Sawney had taught at Horner's School in Oxford, North Carolina, and who attended John's funeral in Bell Buckle in 1916, summarized the essence of John Webb:

---

2. *Address of William Yandell Elliott To The Graduating Class of 1960*, Webb School, Bell Buckle, Tennessee, 90th Commencement, Wednesday, June 8, 1960, 8–10, The Webb School Archives. In an email to this author dated May 29, 2010, Dr. Elliott's son, Ward, recalled that "18 Elliotts have studied under a Webb (and no Webbs under an Elliott), but I'm afraid I wasn't one of them." He had from his father "the impression that Sawney was the stern one and John the gentle one, that Webb boys were 'birched into Latin and wept into Greek.'"

Dr. John Webb was, in my judgment, the most scholarly man engaged in secondary education in the south. I regard him as the most successful and influential teacher of the more advanced pupils of this grade than any man I ever knew. A man of remarkably wide reading, alike in English and foreign literatures, as well as in ancient, he was at the same time as deeply interested in current religious and theological discussions as if this were his special field of study. In full sympathy with modern Biblical scholarship, he read with judicious discrimination and appreciation wellnigh all the new religious books that command the attention of scholarly men. He induced more young preachers to buy and ready new books of real value than any man I have ever known. Modest and retiring in a rare degree, he was yet, underneath his quietness of speech, full of enthusiasm over the things about which he was reading and thinking. One could not be with him for even a few moments without being deeply impressed with the intellectuality, scholarship and deep spirituality of a most unique, gentle, lovable and remarkable man.[3]

Walter Stokes Jr. '09 remembered:

When we became seniors we encountered the gentle encouragement of brother John. Under "Old Jack," as we affectionately called him, we felt the finishing touch of a real scholar. His gentle stimulus encouraged me to read from the shelves of the fine library more Dickens, Shakespeare, Hugo, and Goethe than I have ever read in a similar period since. What a complement to each other were these two brothers "Old Sawney" and "Old Jack"; Sawney the dynamic builder of character coupled with "Old Jack" the gentle inspirer of a literate and cultural life.[4]

---

3. "John M. Webb, Noted Educator, Answers Call," *The Nashville Tennessean and The Nashville American*, Thursday morning, April 6, 1916.

4. An Essay Review by Walter Stokes Jr., of Laurence McMillin's *The Schoolmaker: Sawney Webb and the Bell Buckle Story*, *Tennessee Historical Quarterly*, Vol. XXX, No. 4 (Winter, 1971), 421–422.

Dr. Albert G. Sanders, Webb School Class of 1901 and Rhodes Scholar from Jackson, Mississippi, clarified the contributions of the two brothers:

> The truth surely is that The Webb School was the product of a happy combination of two great teachers whose qualities worked together to produce in the impoverished South a rather remarkable school.[5]

The classic line from Daniel Webster's peroration regarding the 1818–1819 Dartmouth College case is apropos for The Webb School family: "It is, as I have said, a small school; and yet, there are those who love it."[6]

Perhaps it is fitting that Edwin Mims have the last words regarding his old mentor, friend, and confident, John Maurice Webb. Speaking at the 75th Anniversary celebration of The Webb School on June 5, 1946, Dr. Mims spoke of John's journey as the "glory of the unfulfilled life," and he attempted to help his audience understand that those nearest the gentle scholar "'worshipped this side of idolatry'" this quiet, humble scholar. He closed his address with the following:

> My conclusion is that if Mr. Webb had lived in the later years of the Age of Pericles he would have been one of the eager-hearted, intellectually alert Greeks who followed Socrates through the streets of Athens and into the grove of the Academy, discussing such questions as, what is truth, what is justice, what is the good life. And he would have been one who heard the words of the master as he faced death at the hand of the state. If he had lived in the time of Jesus he would have gone, unlike Nicodemus in the night time, to hear of the new birth and of the mysteries of the spirit life; he would have gone like the rich young ruler to ask, "What must I do to inherit eternal life?", but he would not have turned away sorrowfully for he would have taken to heart the answer. Yes, he would have been one of the beloved disciples or even apostles, participating in the

---

5. Holliman, 289.

6. Daniel Webster, Peroration, March 10, 1818, Trustees of Dartmouth College v. Woodward (1819).

Last Supper or suffering with the agony of Gethsemane; yes, he might have been JOHN THE BELOVED.[7]

---

7. Mims, 25.

APPENDIX A

SUGGESTIONS FOR BEGINNING A SCHOOL LIBRARY

by Dr. John M. Webb, Webb School

In accordance with the request of the association, I offer a list of books to form the beginning of a library suitable for secondary schools. In preparing this list I have had before me the needs of Southern schools, especially in rural districts, where there is a dearth of libraries, public and private. The problem is to put into the hands of the susceptible, but untrained, youth a book that will awaken and direct a latent literary taste, hasten the emotions and form character, leading at last to a taste for the world's best literature.

The books are arranged in four groups, aggregating 278 volumes, to cost about $305.

Group A   68 Vols. $50
Webster's International Dictionary.
Harper's Young People Series, 35 vols. (Harper & Bros., New York).

Abbott's Illustrated Histories, 32 vols. (Harper & Bros., New York).

Group B   102 Vols. $80
Century Dictionary of Names.
American Statesmen, 35 vols. (Houghton, Mifflin & Co., Boston).
Little Classics, 16 vols. (Houghton, Mifflin & Co., Boston).
Riverside School Library, 50 vols. (Houghton, Mifflin & Co., Boston).

Group C   100 Vols. $100
Chambers' Cyclopedia, 10 vols.
Lippincott's Gazetteer.
Farrar's Eric, Julian Howe, St. Winifred, 3 vols.
Lanier's Boys' Percy, Boys' King Arthur, Boys' Froissart,
    Knightly Legends, 5 vols.
Eggleston's Beginners of a Nation.
Wilson's George Washington.
Trent's Southern Statesmen.
    "   Robert E. Lee.
White's Robert E. Lee.
Life of Stonewall Jackson, by his Wife.
Cambridge Poets, 5 vols.
Household Poets, 5 vols.
Poems of Lanier, Timrod, Hayne.
Riverside Literature Series, as far as bound in linen, 98 nos. in 61 vols.

Group D   45 Vols. $75
Appleton's Cyclopedia of American Biography, 4 vols.
Lippincott's Biographical Dictionary.
Fiske's Old Virginia and Neighbors, 2 vols.
    "   Critical Period of American History.
    "   American Revolution, 2 vols.
    "   Dutch and Quaker Colonies, 2 vols.
Buckley's Fairy Land of Science
    "   Winners in Life's Race.
    "   Life and Her Children.
Whitney's Life and Growth of Language.
Young's Sun.

APPENDIX A

Judd's Volcanoes.
Bonney's Ice Work.
Gayley's Classic Myths.
Craddock's In Tennessee Mountains.
"   Prophet of Great Smokey Mountains.
"   In the Clouds.
Jas. Lane Allen's Kentucky Cardinal.
" " Aftermath.
" " Choir Invisible.
" " Flute and Violin.
T. N. Page's In the Camps.
" " Old Virginia.
" " Marse Chan.
" " Meh Lady.
" " Red Rock.
Wallace's Ben Hur.
Pyle's Pepper and Salt.
"   Robin Hood.
Monroe's Painted Desert.
"   Rich Dale.
Kipling's Day's Work.
"   From Sea to Sea.
"   Seven Seas.
"   Captain Courageous.
Total, 278 vols. $305.

Source: John M. Webb's only known publication, "School Libraries," was published as part of the *Proceedings of the Sixth Meeting, Association of Colleges and Preparatory Schools of the Southern States* (South Nashville, TN: Publishing House of the Methodist Episcopal Church, 1912), 125–126. The association is now the Southern Association of Colleges and Schools (SACS).

APPENDIX B

THE RHODES SCHOLARS
OF WEBB SCHOOL

Katherine C. Reynolds in *Visions and Vanities: John Andrew Rice and Black Mountain College* (1998) wrote: "In 1904, when the first Rhodes Scholars were named, and for at least twelve years after, competition was not keen." American students favored German universities with its emphasis on graduate study and where one could acquire a PhD degree in three years of study; as a Rhodes Scholar at Oxford, one could add a second bachelor's degree and possibly a master's degree in the same time frame. Also, any applicant to Oxford of the period, including Rhodes Scholars, would have to do well in Responsions, Oxford's entrance examination, which covered Latin and Greek grammar and translation, and mathematics. The staple of Webb School's academic curriculum, potential applicants for the Rhodes Scholarship from the school usually performed quite well in Oxford's Responsions.[1]

---

1. Katherine Chaddock Reynolds, *Visions and Vanities: John Andrew Rice of Black Mountain College* (Baton Rouge, LA: Louisiana State University Press, 1998), 32–33.

Webb's Rhodes Scholars[2]

Note: Eight of the ten Rhodes Scholars educated at Webb School-Bell Buckle were taught by Sawney and John Webb; a ninth Rhodes Scholar attended Webb School prior to Sawney Webb's death in 1926.

G–denotes graduated; NG–attended, non-graduate.

Name	Class	State	Elected
John James Tigrett	Class of 1900 (G)	Tennessee	1904
Albert Godfrey Sanders	Class of 1901 (G)	Texas	1907
Ebb James Ford	Class of 1903 (NG)	Mississippi	1908
Theodore Trimmier McCarley	Class of 1904 (NG)	Mississippi	1908
McDugald [McDougal] Kenneth McLean	Class of 1904 (G)	Texas	1910
John Andrew Rice	Class of 1908 (G)	Louisiana	1911
Hatton Dunnica Towson	Class of 1909 (G)	Georgia	1913
William Yandall Elliott	Class of 1913 (G)	Tennessee	1919
George Tayloe [Taylor] Ross	Class of 1921 (G)	Wyoming	1926
William Webb White	Class of 1950 (G)	Alabama	1954

While Rhodes Scholars Ford (1903) and McCarley (1904) attended Webb School-Bell Buckle, neither graduated from Webb.

The Webb School has produced no further Rhodes Scholars since William Webb White, Class of 1950, of Huntsville, Alabama, a graduate of The University of the South. He is the son of Rhodes Scholar Addison White, who graduated from the University of Alabama in 1907, the same year he was awarded the Rhodes Scholarship.[3]

Other Webb alumni have competed for the Rhodes Scholarship to Oxford University; for example, Inzer B. Wyatt '23, was an alternate Rhodes Scholar and a Phi Beta Kappa graduate of the University of Alabama. A Harvard Law School graduate, he became a U.S. District Judge in New York.[4]

---

2. Thomas J. and Kathleen Schaeper, *Cowboys Into Gentlemen: Rhodes Scholars, Oxford, and the Creation of An American Elite* (New York: Berghahn Books, 1998), 360–368.

3. *Alabama Alumni Magazine* (August–September 1995), 29.

4. The Webb School Archives, Bell Buckle, Tennessee.

APPENDIX C

DID JOHN WEBB SERVE IN THE CONFEDERACY?

It has been assumed that John Webb was too young for service in the Civil War (though many younger boys certainly served) and that, as a student cadet in 1865 at Bingham School in Mebanesville (Mebane, 1883), North Carolina, probably only saw guard duty at best. However, the *Alumni History of The University of North Carolina*, 2nd edition, 1924, page 653, lists John Maurice Webb as a lieutenant in Co. A, 3rd Battalion, CSA, in his alumni record.[1]

John Andrew Rice claimed that John Webb "had been too young to be taken to war and…remained a student at the University of North Carolina."[2] However, UNC alumni records state that John was a student there after the war from 1866 to 1868, for a period of about two

---

1. Daniel Lindsey Grant, *Alumni History of The University of North Carolina*, 2nd ed. (Durham, NC: Christian & King Printing Co., 1924), 653.

2. Rice, 199.

and a half years. John was a student at Bingham School from 1862–1864 at Oaks, and a student cadet at Bingham School in Mebanesville from December 1864 onward.

The multi-volume history of North Carolina units in the Civil War lists a John M. Webb, Second Lieutenant, Co. A, Third Battalion (Light Artillery). The company was recruited in Northampton County, North Carolina, and Company A was one of three batteries in the battalion.[3]

The only John M. Webb who served in a North Carolina unit, this Webb was a twenty-year old born in Northampton County, who enlisted on January 30, 1862, in Northampton County, as a second lieutenant. He was commissioned into Company A, North Carolina 3rd Battalion Light Artillery on February 10, 1862. John Webb was still on the rolls on December 31, 1864, and was paroled on April 27, 1865, at Greensboro, North Carolina (though he was absent and sick at home when paroled).[4]

Thus it appears that the University of North Carolina incorrectly listed John Maurice Webb in his alumni record as a Confederate artillerist, presumably taken from lists of soldiers serving in the Confederacy from North Carolina.

Finally, data contained in a "Find a Grave" entry for William Robert Webb ["Sawney"] states that John Maurice Webb served in [Captain Edward D.] Snead's (Sneed's) Company of [North Carolina] Local Defense militia, entering service on January 1, 1864, after his sixteenth birthday on November 29 [27], 1863. Bingham School moved from Oaks to Mebanesville (Mebane), North Carolina, in December 1864; prevailing evidence suggests that John Webb remained a student cadet at the school until the end of the Civil War.[5]

---

3. Major John W. Moore, "Third Battalion (Light Artillery)," *Histories of the Several Regiments and Battalions from North Carolina in the Great War 1861–'65*, ed. by Walter Clark, Vol. IV, Published by The State (Goldsboro, NC: Nash Brothers, Book and Job Printers, 1901), 261.

4. Data courtesy of Nicholas P. Picerno, Chief of Police and Campus Security, Bridgewater College, Bridgewater, Virginia, from his Civil War database (Confederate soldiers), February 8, 2013.

5. Find a Grave: "William Robert Webb." http://www.findagrave.com/cig-bin/fg.cgi?page=fl s&FLid=58505811&FLgrid=793166

APPENDIX D

THE SANBORN-PERRIS FIRE INSURANCE MAPS OF BELL BUCKLE, TENNESSEE 1894–1924

From June 1894 to April 1924, the Sanborn-Perris Map Company (later Sanborn Map Company) of New York City produced some eleven maps of Bell Buckle, Tennessee, particularly for fire insurance purposes. Maps were produced for June 1894 (1), December 1899 (1), July 1907 (1), September 1914 (2), and April 1924 (3, 3–501).

Nearly every structure of note is recorded, the maps depicting the business block (Rail Road Square), hotel, bank (later two banks), passenger and freight depots, stock yard, mills, and other outlying commercial businesses, with Main Street running due east past Webb School. The school itself, "Webb's School," one-third of a mile east of the depot, is included as an insert to the maps which varies very little from the 1894, 1899, 1907, and 1914 maps.

The insert for Webb School shows the Big Room and the "Library" (Senior Room) next to Main Street. However the Junior Room, sitting southeast of the Big Room, is just outside the frame of the insert and is not depicted in any of the Sanborn-Perris maps through 1914.

While some speculation claims that the Junior Room wasn't depicted in the 1894 map because it had yet to be built, the Junior Room was indeed constructed in 1886 at about the same time as the Big Room and the Senior Room/Library.

The September 1914 and April 1924 maps show Maple Street with the Methodist Episcopal (M.E.) Church, South, and the homes of Sawney and John Webb across the street from each other.

The insert for Webb School in the 1924 maps is drawn from a little different perspective than the earlier maps and the Junior Room is shown but listed only as "Class R'M."

Population figures for Bell Buckle included on the maps for 1894–1924, listed 1,000 people for June 1894; 900 for December 1899; 1,100 for July 1907; 1,000 for September 1914; and only 500 for April 1924.

> *Source*: Environmental Data Sources—Digital Sanborn Maps (commercial database), courtesy of Mike Klein, Geography and Map Division, Library of Congress, Washington, D.C., March 1, 2013. Thanks also to William B. Eigelsbach, Special Collections, Hodges Library, University of Tennessee, Knoxville, for fetchimage data from the April 1924 maps, June 25, 2013, and to Sue Alexander of the James E. Walker Library at Middle Tennessee State University, Murfreesboro, for a fetchimage of an April 1924 map, June 28, 2013.

APPENDIX D   133

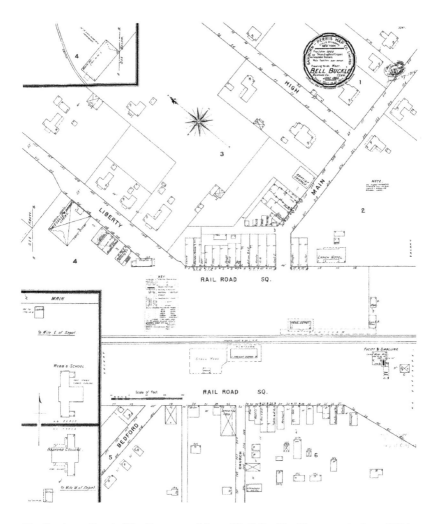

The Sanborn-Perris Fire Insurance Map of Bell Buckle, Tennessee in June 1894, showing Webb School in an insert. The Big Room faced due west parallel to the Main Road, and the Library (Senior Room) faced the Main Road. The Junior Room is not included in this insert, but it does appear in the 1924 maps. (Courtesy of Environmental Data Resources [Digital Sanborn Maps])

APPENDIX E

SOME ASSISTANT TEACHERS AT WEBB SCHOOL (BELL BUCKLE) 1888–1912

From the Webb School letterheads located in the Edwin Mims Papers at Vanderbilt University, below is a listing, however incomplete overall, with the dates of the letters for teaching assistants who served with Principals W.R. Webb, AM; John M. Webb, AM; and later, W.R. Webb Jr., AB. The names are listed just as they appear on the letterheads.

August 25, 1888—Jas. D. Clary; Rev. G.L. Beale, AM; R.G. Peoples
November 23, 1903—W.R. Webb Jr., AB; Ed. T. Price;
    W.L. Clarke, AB; F.W. Whiteside
March 15, 1907—W.R. Webb Jr., AB; W.L. Clarke, AB;
    Robert Proctor; McD. K. McLean
April 5, 1907—W.R. Webb Jr., AB; W.L. Clarke, AB;
    Robert Proctor; McD. K. McLean

December 25, 1907—W.R. Webb Jr., AB; Will Alf. Jacobs, AB; John T. Clary

January 10, 1908—W.R. Webb Jr., AB; Will Alf. Jacobs, AB; John T. Clary

January 5, 1911—The three Principals including W. R. Webb Jr., AB. *Assistants*: E.T. Price, AB; M.K. M'Lean, AB; H.B. Shofner

February 22, 1912—The three Principals including W.R. Webb Jr., AB. *Assistants*: H.B. Shofner; G.H. Armistead Jr.; C.D. Stephenson.

BIBLIOGRAPHY

Printed Materials

Adams, Henry. *The Education of Henry Adams*. Boston, MA: Houghton Mifflin, 1961.
Address of William Yandell Elliott To The Class of 1960, Webb School, Bell Buckle, Tennessee, 90th Commencement, June 8, 1960.
Alumni Directory, The Webb School, 1984. Bell Buckle, TN: The Alumni Association of The Webb School, 1984.
Annual Catalogue of Trinity College, 1917–1918; 1921–1922. Durham, NC: Trinity College.
Barr, Charlotte. *The Bell Buckle Years*. Bell Buckle, TN: Iris Press, 1992.
Barringer, Paul B. *The Natural Bent: The Memoirs of Dr. Paul B. Barringer*. Chapel Hill, NC: The University of North Carolina Press, 1949.

Batts, William O. *Private Preparatory Schools for Boys in Tennessee, Since 1867.* Columbia, TN: Privately published, 1957.

Beavers, David R. *A History of Banks of Bedford County, Tennessee, 1807-1983.* Privately printed, October 1987.

Bedford County, Tennessee. Memphis, TN: Books LLC, 2010.
"Bell Buckle, Tennessee" (5–8)
"Webb School (Bell Buckle, Tennessee)" (27–30)

Chandler, David Leon, with Mary Voelz Chandler. *The Binghams of Louisville: The Dark History Behind One of America's Great Fortunes.* New York: Crown Publishers, Inc., 1987.

Conkin, Paul K. *Gone With the Ivy: A Biography of Vanderbilt University.* Knoxville, TN: The University of Tennessee Press, 1985.

Curtis, Robert I. "The Bingham School and Classical Education in North Carolina, 1793–1873." *The North Carolina Historical Review.* Vol. LXXIII, No. 3 (July 1996), 329–377.

Davidson, Donald. *The Tennessee: Volume II: The New River, Civil War To TVA.* Rivers of America Series. New York: Rinehart & Company, Inc., 1948.

Doors to the Past: Homes of Shelbyville and Bedford County. Bedford County Historical Society. Shelbyville, TN: *The Shelbyville Times-Gazette*, 1969.

Duberman, Martin. *Black Mountain: An Exploration in Community.* New York: E. P. Dutton & Co., Inc., 1972.

Durden, Robert F. *The Launching of Duke University, 1924–1949.* Durham, NC: Duke University Press, 1993.

Elliott, Randolph. "Old Sawney's." *The Atlantic Monthly* (August 1920), 231–236.

Fremantle, Lt. Col. Arthur J. L. *Three Months in the Southern States, April-June, 1863.* Introduction by Gary G. Gallagher. Lincoln, NE: University of Nebraska Press (Bison Books), 1991. Reprint of the 1864 edition.

Grant, Daniel Lindsey. *Alumni History of The University of North Carolina.* 2nd ed. Durham, NC: Christian & King Printing Co., 1924.

Harris, Mary Emma. *The Arts of Black Mountain College.* Cambridge, MA: MIT Press, 1987.

Holliman, Glenn N. "The Webb School Junior Room, The Symbol of a School." *Tennessee Historical Quarterly.* Vol. 36, No. 3 (Fall 1977), 287–304.

Kreyling, Christine, et al. *Classical Nashville: Athens of the South.* Nashville, TN: Vanderbilt University Press, 1996.

Link, Arthur S., ed. *The Papers of Woodrow Wilson.* Vol. 16, 1905–1907. Princeton, NJ: Princeton University Press, 1973.

Locke, Mildred, Compiler/Writer. *Bell Buckle United Methodist Church: 100 Years, 1883–1993; Est. 1807.* Bell Buckle, TN: The compiler, 1993.

Lord, Walter, ed. and commentary. *The Fremantle Diary, Being the Journal of Lieutenant Colonel Arthur James Lyon Fremantle, Coldstream Guards, On His Three Months in the Southern States.* Boston, MA: Little, Brown and Company, 1954.

Lynch, Louise Gillespie, compiler and publisher. *Death Records of Bedford County, Tennessee, 1984.* Franklin, TN: L. G. Lynch, 1984.

Marsh, Helen C. and Timothy R., compilers. *Cemetery Records of Bedford County, Tennessee. Revised 1985, Shelbyville, Tennessee.* Easley, SC: Southern Historical Press, Inc., 1986.

Marsh, Helen C. and Timothy R., compilers. *Official Marriages of Bedford County, Tennessee, 1861–1880, Vol. 1.* Greenville, SC: Southern Historical Press, Inc., 1996.

McLean, Emma Webb. *Sawney Webb: Maker of Men.* Privately published. Laverne, CA: Preston Printing, 1969.

McMillin, Laurence. *The Schoolmaker: Sawney Webb & the Bell Buckle Story.* Chapel Hill, NC: The University of North Carolina Press, 1971. Special Webb School reprint, 1995.

McMillin, Laurence. Sawney Webb: Southern Schoolmaster, A Case History of Individualism in American Education. Thesis (MA). Claremont, CA: Claremont Graduate School, 1960.

McTyeire, Holland N. *Hymn Book of the Methodist Episcopal Church, South.* Nashville, TN: Publishing House of the M. E. Church, South, J.D. Barbee, Agent, 1889.

Mims, Edwin. *Chancellor Kirkland of Vanderbilt.* Nashville, TN: Vanderbilt University Press, 1940.

Mims, Edwin. *History of Vanderbilt University.* Nashville, TN: Vanderbilt University Press, 1946.

Mims, Edwin. "John Maurice Webb, 1847–1916." An address delivered at Webb School commencement, June 5, 1946, in connection with the 75th anniversary of the founding of Webb School. Nashville, TN: [s.n.], 1946.

"Most Famous Educator of the South." *Confederate Veteran* (March 1927), 86–87.

"Paint Analysis of the Junior Room, Webb School, Bell Buckle, Tennessee, August 1976," by Building Conservation Technology, Inc., and submitted to Architect-Engineer Associates, Inc., Nashville, Tennessee. Project funded by a matching grant from the Department of the Interior under the

National Historic Preservation Act of 1966. Webb School, Junior Room, Development Project # 477600129-00.

Parks, Edd Winfield. "Sawney Webb: Tennessee's Schoolmaster." *North Carolina Historical Review*. Vol. 12, No. 3 (July 1935), 233–251.

Parks, Edd Winfield. *Segments of Southern Thought*. Athens, GA: The University of Georgia Press, 1938.

"Past is Prologue." *The Webb School Alumni Directory, 1988*. Bell Buckle, TN: The Webb School, 1988.

Porter, Earl W. *Trinity and Duke, 1892–1924: Foundations of Duke University*. Durham, NC: Duke University Press, 1964.

Postcard Memories of Bedford County, Tennessee. Bicentennial Celebration 2007. Published by the Bedford County Historical Society, Shelbyville, Tennessee. Nashville, TN: Panacea Press, 2006.

Powell, William Stevens, ed. *Dictionary of North Carolina Biography*. 6 vols. Chapel Hill: The University of North Carolina Press, 1979-1996. Vol. 1 (A–C), 1979; Vol. 2 (D–G), 1986; Vol. 3 (H–K), 1988; Vol. 4 (L–O), 1991; Vol. 5 (P–S), 1994; Vol. 6 (T–Z), 1996.

Proceedings of the Annual Meetings, Association of Colleges and Preparatory Schools of the Southern States, 1895–1911 (now Southern Association of Colleges and Schools). Nashville, TN: The Association, 1912.

Proceedings of the Sixth Meeting, Association of Colleges and Preparatory Schools of the Southern States (now Southern Association of Colleges and Schools). South Nashville, TN: Publishing House of the Methodist Episcopal Church, 1912.

Report of the President of Trinity College to the Board of Trustees, June, 1918, Durham, North Carolina.

Reynolds, Katherine Chaddock. *Visions and Vanities: John Andrew Rice of Black Mountain College*. Baton Rouge, LA: Louisiana State University Press, 1998.

Rice, John Andrew. *I Came Out of the Eighteenth Century*. New York: Harper & Brothers, 1942.

Rice, John Andrew. "Two Schoolteachers." *Harper's Magazine* 184 (January 1942), 201–209.

Robbins, David P. *Century Review of Maury County, Tennessee, 1805–1905*. Columbia, TN: Auspices of the Board of Mayor and Aldermen, 1906.

Sain, Lynne, and Linda Vannatta, Compilers. *Potluck Pickins' and Picturesque Places of Bell Buckle, Tennessee.* Bell Buckle, TN: The Daffodilly, n.d. [19–]

Schaeper, Thomas J. and Kathleen. *Cowboys Into Gentlemen: Rhodes Scholars, Oxford, and the Creation of An American Elite.* New York: Berghahn Books, 1998.

"School Bells at Bell Buckle." *Southern Living* (October 1979), 44.

Sistler, Byron and Barbara, Preparers. *1880 Census—Tennessee, Transcription for Maury County.* Nashville, TN: B. Sistler, 1994.

Snavely, Guy E. "A Short History of the Southern Association of Colleges and Secondary Schools." Executive Director, Association of American Colleges. Durham, NC, 1945.

"Specifications For Restoration of Webb School Junior Room, Project No. 47-76-00129-00, October 6, 1976," presented by Architect-Engineer Associates, Nashville, Tennessee.

Stokes, Walter Jr. "The Schoolmaker: Sawney Webb & the Bell Buckle Story." *Tennessee Historical Quarterly.* Vol. 30, No. 4 (Winter 1971), 419–422. (Essay review)

The Tennessee Magazine (October 1986). Nashville, TN: Tennessee Electric Cooperative Association. (Cover image of the Junior Room)

"The Three Governors From Webb School—Each An Individual." *The Webb School, Alumni Bulletin* (Fall 1977), 3–5.

Tilley, Nannie M. *The Trinity College Historical Society, 1892–1941.* Durham, NC: Duke University Press, 1941.

"The Tullahoma Campaign—Communities—Bell Buckle." http://mtweb.mtsu.edu/tullproj/Communities/bell_buckle.html.

Turner, William Bruce. *History of Maury County, Tennessee.* Nashville, TN: Parthenon Press, 1955.

Van West, Carroll, editor-in-chief. *The Tennessee Encyclopedia of History and Culture.* Tennessee Historical Society. Nashville, TN: Rutledge Hill Press, 1998.

"Webb School" by A. Jon Frere, 1043

"Webb, William R. 'Sawney' (1842-1926)" by Ridley Wills II, 1044

Vaughn, Maggi. *Season It With Bell Buckle.* Bell Buckle, TN: Bell Buckle Press, 1991.

Waldrop, Frank C., ed. *Mountain Voices: The Centennial History of Monteagle Sunday School Assembly.* Nashville, TN: The Parthenon Press, 1982.

Washington and Lee University Alumni Directory, 1749–1985. Class of 1870. White Plains, NY: Bernard C. Harris Publishing Company, Inc., 1986.

"Webb, John Maurice." *Who's Who in America, 1916-1917.* Vol. 9 (Chicago: A.N. Marquis & Co., 1916), 2603.

Webb School in Celebration of its 75th Birthday. Foreword by William R. Webb, Jr., 1945.

Webb, W.J. and others. *Our Webb Kin of Dixie: A Family History.* Oxford, NC: W. J. Webb, 1940.

Webb, William R. "Sawney Webb: My Father and His Ideals for Education." *The Sewanee Review*, No. 2 (April 1942), 227–240.

"The Webbs of Bell Buckle." Education section, *Time* (September 16, 1946), 75.

White, Robert Hiram. *Development of the Tennessee State Educational Organization, 1796–1929.* Kingsport, TN: Southern Publishers, 1929.

"Who are The Rhodes Scholars of Webb School?" *The Webb School, Alumni Bulletin* (Spring 1977), 3–6.

Williamson, Samuel R. Jr., and Smith, Gerald L., with Tracey W. Omohundro. Preface by John M. McCardell Jr. *Yea, Sewanee's Right! A Pictorial History of The University of the South. A publication of the Sewanee History Project.* Sewanee, TN: The University of the South, 2011.

York, Max. "They've Saved Sawney's Room." *The Tennessean* (Sunday, November 27, 1977), 1–2 F ("Panorama").

Archival Sources and Special Collections

Claremont University Consortium, Claremont, California
    Honnold/Mudd Library
    Claremont Colleges Library
        Thesis (MA) by Laurence McMillin, 1960

Duke University, Durham, North Carolina
    Duke University Archives
    David M. Rubenstein Rare Book and Manuscript Library
        Trinity College Library Accession Books
        Albert M. Webb File

Library of Congress, Washington, DC
    Geography and Map Division
        Sanborn Fire Maps of Bell Buckle, Tennessee

Middle Tennessee State University, Murfreesboro, Tennessee
    James E. Walker Library
        Nashville newspapers on microfilm
        1924 Sanborn Fire Maps of Bell Buckle, Tennessee
University of North Carolina, Chapel Hill, North Carolina
    Louis Round Wilson Special Collections Library
    Southern Historical Collection:
        Benjamin Cudworth Yancey Papers, M-2594, Reels 12 & 13.
        The Webb Family Papers (Webb-Moore Papers), Reel 1
        Leak-Wall Papers, SHC # 1468, Vol. S-1
The University of the South, Sewanee, Tennessee
    University Archives and Special Collections
        Dr. John Maurice Webb II File
Tennessee State Library and Archives, Nashville, Tennessee
        The Tennessee Teacher
University of Tennessee, Knoxville, Tennessee
    Special Collections
    Hodges Library
        1924 Sanborn Fire Maps of Bell Buckle, Tennessee
Vanderbilt University, Nashville, Tennessee
    Special Collections and University Archives
    Vanderbilt University Library
        Edwin Mims Papers
University of Virginia, Charlottesville, Virginia
    Albert and Shirley Small Special Collections Library
    University of Virginia Library
        William Bingham publications (Confederate Imprint)
The Webb School, Bell Buckle, Tennessee
    William Bond Library
    The Webb School Archives

Newspapers

Asheville Citizen, January 2, 1927
Durham Morning Herald, September 9, 1965
The Columbia Herald, January 24, 1873
The Nashville Banner, November 27, 1905, January 13, 1912

The Nashville Tennessean and *The Nashville American*, April 6–9, 1916
Raleigh News and Observer, June 30, 1929
The Shelbyville Times-Gazette, April 13, 1916
Trinity Chronicle, October 31, 1917, December 14, 1921

Libraries and Historical Societies

Argie Cooper Library, Shelbyville, Tennessee
    Local History and Genealogy
Bedford County Historical Society, Shelbyville, Tennessee
Birmingham Public Library, Birmingham, Alabama
    Tutwiler Collection of Southern History and Literature
Durham County Library, Durham, North Carolina
    North Carolina Collection
Huntsville-Madison County Public Library, Huntsville, Alabama
    Heritage Room
Jacksonville Public Library, Jacksonville, Alabama
    History Room
Jacksonville State University, Jacksonville, Alabama
    Houston Cole Library
Nashville Public Library, Nashville, Tennessee
Olivia Raney Library, Raleigh, North Carolina
Richmond County Historical Society, Rockingham, North Carolina

INDEX

A

Abernathy, Kimi, xx
Abernathy Street (Bell Buckle, TN), 116
Academic Hall, University of Virginia, 75
"Academical village," University of Virginia, 17
Academy (Plato), 121
Achilles, 82
Adams, Henry, 64
Adult education, 77–79
The Advancing South (1926), 63
Aegean Isles, 82
African American enrollment, The Webb School (Bell Buckle, TN), 71–72
African Americans, 6, 22, 27, 71–72
Africans, 72

Agrarians (literary movement), 5, 63
Alabama, 27, 116
Alabama A&M University, xix, xx
Alamance County, North Carolina, 6, 7, 10–11
Alaska, 30
Albert M. Shipp Library (Trinity College), 102–103
Alcohol, 22–23, 25, 27, 29–30
Alexander Mack Library (Bridgewater College), xx
Alley, James G., 56
Almeda Schoolhouse, 7
"An Act to Incorporate Bingham School" (North Carolina General Assembly), 9–11

Alumni and Public Relations, Webb
    School (Bell Buckle, TN),
    129–130
*Alumni History of The University of
    North Carolina* (2nd ed., 1924),
    129–130
Alzheimer's Disease, xx
Ambassador, U.S., 8, 9, 15, 66–67
Ambassador-at-Large, U.S., 67
Amelia Courthouse, Virginia, 12
American Bar Association, 99
American flag, 109
American Medal of Freedom, 68
American Red Cross, 67, 106
American Rhodes Scholarships, xviii
American University, 5
Annual Bike Rally & Poker Run
    Festival (Bell Buckle, TN), 116
Annual Catalogue of Trinity College
    (1917–1918), 100
    (1921–1922), 103
Anti-Prohibitionists, 30
Appomattox Courthouse, Virginia, 14,
    18
Arcadia Press, xix, xx
Arkansas, 50–51
Arkansas Brigade, CSA, 50–51
Aristocrats (English), 61
Aristotle, 44
Armour, Annie, ix, 108
Armistead, G.H. Jr., 136
Armstrong, Walter, 99–100
Army of Northern Virginia, CSA, 14, 51
Army of Tennessee, CSA, 51
Army-Navy football game, 70
The Arts at Black Mountain College
    (1987), 5, 85–86
Asheville, North Carolina, 11, 15, 69,
    110
Assistant teachers, Webb School
    (Bell Buckle, TN), 135–136
Association of American Colleges, 73,
    76
Association of Colleges and Preparatory/Secondary Schools of the
    Southern States, 63, 75–76
Athens, Georgia, 47, 75
Athens, Greece, 75, 121

"Athens of the South" (Nashville, TN),
    75
Athletic field, Webb School (Bell Buckle,
    TN), 45
Athletics. *See* Sports
Atlanta, Georgia, 49, 51, 68, 75
The Atlantic Monthly (1920), 4, 81–82
Attorney General, U.S., 30
Austin Davis-Bryant Woosley
    Computer/Science Building, 45
Automobiles, 43
Aydelotte, Frank, 83

B

Baer Memorial Library (Marion, AL), xx
Baliol College (Oxford), 119
Baltimore, Maryland, 106
Bank of Bell Buckle, 3, 50, 56–57,
    104–105, 115
Baptists, 78
Barringer, General Paul, 11
Barringer, Paul B., 11
Barringer, General Rufus Clay, 11
Bassett, John Spencer, 88–89
"The Batch," 24, 37
Battle Creek, Michigan, viii, 55
Battleground Academy, 69
Bayonets, 50
Beale, George L., 45, 135
Bedford College, 83, 114–115
Bedford County, Tennessee, 29, 49, 98,
    109, 114
Bedford County Draft Exemption
    Board, 109
Bell Buckle, Tennessee, xvi, xvii, xviii, xix,
    3, 29, 49–52, 93, 115, 132
"Bellbuckle," 47, 50, 95
Bell Buckle Cafe, 115
Bell Buckle Creek, 49–50, 115
"Bell Buckle Historic District," 116
Bell Buckle Post Office, 115
Bell Buckle United Methodist Church,
    58–59, 116, 132
Benjamin Cudworth Yancey Papers,
    Southern Historical Collection,
    UNC, 28–29, 46–48, 143

Bethlehem Presbyterian Church/
    Cemetery (Oaks, NC), 7, 17–18
Biblical scholarship/studies, 5, 25–26, 37,
    59, 76–77, 96, 118, 120
Bicycling, 48, 56
Big Room (schoolhouse), Bell Buckle,
    TN, xxv, 34–38, 41–42, 45–47,
    53, 72, 81, 131–133
"Big Room," Eton College, 61
Bingham family, 6–9, 14
Bingham Hall, UNC, 15
"Bingham Heights" (Asheville, NC), 15
Bingham home (Oaks, NC), 8–9
Bingham, Mary Lily Kenan Flagler
    (Mrs. Robert Worth Bingham),
    16
Bingham Military School (Asheville,
    NC), 11, 15, 69
Bingham Military School, Board of
    Trustees, 15
Bingham, Robert (1838–1927), 11,
    14–15, 69
Bingham, Robert Worth (1871–1937),
    9, 15–16
Bingham School (Mebane, NC), xix, 3,
    7, 10–14, 18–19, 31, 75, 129–130
Bingham School (Oaks, NC), xix, 3, 7,
    10, 12–14, 31, 38, 75, 129–130
Bingham, William (1754–1826), 8
Bingham, William (1835–1873), 10–11,
    14, 19
Bingham, William James (1802–1866),
    7–10, 14
Bingham's Latin Grammar, 10
Birmingham-Southern College, 66
Black Mountain College, xvi, 5, 66, 86
Blacks (African Americans), 6, 22, 71–72
Blue Ridge, North Carolina, 110
Boarding houses, 9, 12, 22, 24, 26, 28, 37,
    46–47, 72
Boarding students, 9–12, 22, 24, 26, 28,
    37, 46–47, 72
Bond, William, 108–109
Book Club (Shelbyville, TN), 77, 98
Bradley A/V Building, The Webb School
    (Bell Buckle, TN), 45
Bragg, Braxton, 51
Branham & Hughes School, 69

Brethren Historical Library and
    Archives (BHLA), xx
Bridgewater, Virginia, xx
Bridgewater College, xx, 130
Brodnax, James, 71
Brooks, Cleanth, 63
"Brother Sawney," 104
Brothers Grimm, xv, xvi
Browning, 60, 96
Brownsville, Texas, 51
Bryn Mawr College, 68
Bugscuffle, Tennessee, 114

C

Caesar's Commentaries on the Gallic Wars
    (1864), 10
California, 69, 119
Camp Chase, Ohio (Union prison), 12
Caney Fork River, Tennessee, 59
Cannon, James III, 107
Carmack, Edward W. (Ned), 30
Carnegie Units, 76, 85, 89
Cave Hill Cemetery (Louisville, KY), 16
"The Celebration" (Shelbyville, TN), 114
Census, U.S., 20, 27
Centennial Club (Nashville, TN), 77
Center Point, Virginia, 11
Century Review of Maury County,
    Tennessee, 1805–1905 (1906),
    22–23
Chambers, Jack, 43
Chambliss Dormitory, xviii, 45
Chancery Court of Tennessee, 30
Chancellor Kirkland of Vanderbilt (1940),
    63, 67
Chapel Hill, North Carolina, 7–8, 12, 14,
    17–18, 20, 26, 29, 46, 61, 109
Chappell, Edwin B., 27
Charleston, South Carolina, xix, 51
Charlotte, North Carolina, 68
Charlottesville, Virginia, 17, 75–76
Chatham Academy, 8
Chattanooga, Tennessee, 49, 51, 107, 114
Chautauqua Institute (New York), 78
Chautauqua Lake Sunday School
    Assembly, 78

"Chautauqua of the South," Monteagle Assembly, Tennessee, 78–79
Cherokee Indians, 50
Chicago Symphony Orchestra, 106
Chief of Police (Bell Buckle, TN), 115
Chief of Police (Bridgewater College), 130
Chinese, 66, 72
Choctaw Indians, 28, 71
Cholera, 24
Christian ministry, 30, 56
Christmas, 48
Cincinnati, Ohio, 78
City Point, Virginia (Union prison), 11
Civil War, 9, 10–11, 14, 18, 23, 50, 130
Claremont, California, 119
Claremont McKenna College, 69, 119
Clarke, C.C., 74
Clarke, W.L., 135
Mrs. Clarke's School for Girls, 25
Clary, Alla B., 23, 27
Clary, Benjamin, 23
Clary, James D., 135
Clary, John T., 136
Clary, Mary Lee, 73
Clary, William F., 33–34
Class of 1903 gift, Webb School (Bell Buckle, TN), 44
Class of 1960, Webb School, Bell Buckle, TN (Elliott address), 119
Classical Department, Phillips Academy, 67
Classical schools, 8, 9, 26, 32, 71, 82
Classics, 28, 82–83
Cleburne, Patrick, 51
Cleveland, Frances (Folsom), 48
Cleveland, Grover, 48
"The Club" (Bell Buckle, TN), 77
Coeducation, 71–72
Coker, Frank, 34
H.M. Coldstream Guards, 50
College Football Hall of Fame, 67
College of William and Mary in Virginia, 65
College preparation, 31–32
Columbia, South Carolina, 75–76
Columbia, Tennessee, 23
Columbia University, 65

Commissioner of Education, U.S., 66
Computer/Science Building, The Webb School (Bell Buckle, TN), 45
The Confederacy, 10–12
Congressman, U.S., 68
Cooper, Jim, 66
Cooper, William Prentice Sr., 66
Cooper, William Prentice Jr., 66
Cornell University, 63
"Couldn't Hear Nobody Pray" (Negro spiritual), 58
Country Music, 30
Court of St. James, England, 9, 15
Covington, Benjamin Harrison, 20
Covington family, 20
Covington, Mary Ann (Harlee), 20
Crawford, William P., 115
Crawford's General Merchandise Store, (Bell Buckle, TN), 115
Creationism, 77
Creative writing, 63
Crenshaw, Dorothy (Mullins), 55
Crenshaw, Jim, 55
Critical thinking, xvi, 80
Culleoka, Tennessee, xix, 4, 17, 21–31, 58, 60, 64, 66, 71
Culleoka Academy, 11, 21, 23, 25, 28–30, 34, 36, 60, 66, 71, 112–113
Culleoka Institute, 11, 21, 23, 26, 28, 60, 66, 71, 113
Culleoka Post Office, 112, 114
Culleoka School (K–12), 30
Cumberland Plateau, 78
Curriculum, Culleoka, TN, 26–27
Curriculum, Bell Buckle, TN, 37, 51, 85, 117
Curtis, T.R., 95

D

"The Daffadilly" (Bell Buckle, TN), 115
Dante, 77–78, 101, 118–119
Dante class (Murfreesboro, TN), 77–78
Dante Club (Bell Buckle, TN), 77
Dartmouth v. Woodward (1818–1819), 121
Davidson College, 11
Davidson, Donald, 63

Davis, Ewin L., 68
Davis, Norman H., 67
Day students, xv, 55
Dean, H.E., 115
Dean's Drug Store (Bell Buckle, TN), 115
Debaters, 18, 60
Debating, 18, 60
Democratic National Committee, 67
Democratic Party, 67
The Great Depression, 52, 57
Deserters (Confederate), 14
Dewey, John, 91
Dewey Decimal System, 44, 101
Dialectic Society, UNC, 18
Dickens, 120
Digital Sanborn Maps (commercial database), 132–133
Dinwiddie, A.G., 21
"Distinction," 47
District Attorney, U.S., 30
District Judge, U.S. (New York), 128
The Divine Comedy, 77
Dixie Flyer, 94–95
Dockery, Mary, 20
Doctor of Laws (LLD, Honorary), 73, 75
Duck River, Tennessee, 49, 51
Due West, South Carolina, 109
Duke Divinity School Library, 101–102
Duke Medical Center (Durham, NC), 107
Duke University, 65, 101, 103, 107–108
Duke University Archives, 100
Duncan School, 69
Duncan, T.J., 59
Durham, North Carolina, 76, 100, 107–108
Durham County Library, NC, 107
Durham Herald-Sun, 107
Durham Morning Herald, 100, 107

E

Education, compulsory, 15
Education, teacher, 15
Education, women's, 15
The Education of Henry Adams (1919), 64
Eigelsbach, William B., 132
Elgin, Illinois, xx

Elkins, Dorothy P., 72
Elliott, Eddie, 82
Elliott family, 82
Elliott, Ida A., 41, 82
Elliott, Randolph, 4, 41, 81–82
Elliott, Ward, 119
Elliott, William Yandell, 5, 6, 118–119, 128
Elmira, New York (Union prison), 12
Elysian Fields, 5, 82
Emory University, 65, 88
Enfield rifles, 50
England, xviii, 8–9
English, 9, 26, 28, 60–63, 78, 82, 85
English aristocrats, 61
English grammar, 26
English literature, 43, 60, 78, 101
English public school (private), 61
Erskine College, 109
Eton College, 61
Europe, 60–61
Evolution, 76

F

Farrar, Alfred, 43
Fasti of Ovid, 48
Faxon, Russ, 115
Federal Trade Commission, 68
Female boarding students, 58, 71
Fifteenth North Carolina Infantry Regiment (Company H), CSA, 11
Fiftieth Annual Public Debate (Webb School debating societies), 60
Fighting, fist, 29
"Find a Grave," 130
Fist fighting, 29
Fitzgerald & Clarke School, 69
Flag, American, 109
Flagler, Henry M., 16
Flagler, Mary Lily (Kenan), 16 *See* Mrs. Robert Worth Bingham
Florida, 16
Florence, Italy, 107
Florence, South Carolina, 107
Follin, Gerald Webb Sr., 62, 110
"Follow the Gleam," Centennial Club, 77

Ford, Ebb J., 128
Fort Delaware, Delaware (Union prison), 12, 14
Forty-seventh Regiment, North Carolina Militia, CSA, 14
Forty-fourth North Carolina Infantry (Company G), CSA, 14
Fountain Creek (Culleoka, TN), 24, 113
France, 103, 119
Franklin, Tennessee, 25
Freemantle, Arthur James Lyon, 50
French, 26, 48, 74, 82
French Broad River, 14
Frere, A. Jon, xx, 32
Frere, Penny, xx
Fugitives (literary movement), 5, 63
Fugitt, Alfred D., 33, 49–50
Fundamentalism, 76

G

Gambia, 72
Garland, Landon C., 32
Geneva Conference (1933), 67
"Gentle scholar." *See* John Maurice Webb
Gentlemen, 61
George Beale Building (Junior Room), 45
George Peabody College for Teachers, 75
German, 26, 48, 82, 85
German universities, 127
Gethsemane (Jesus), 121–122
Gettysburg, Pennsylvania, 51
Gibson, Betty, 112
Gibson, Leonard, 112
Gillespie Cemetery (Wallace, SC), 102–103
Goethe, 120
Goucher College, 106
Grady, Henry W., 47
Grammar, English, 10, 26
A Grammar of the English Language (1867), 10
A Grammar of the Latin Language (1863), 10
Grand Ole Opry, 30, 115
Great Britain, 8–9, 15–16

Greece, 75, 121
Greek, 7, 9, 13, 24, 26, 43, 51, 71, 82, 85–86, 101, 118–119, 127
Greek Club (Vanderbilt University), 77
Greek Department (Randolph-Macon Woman's College), 68
Greek New Testament, 118
Greek Play Tradition (Randolph-Macon Woman's College), 68
Greeks, 121
Greensboro, North Carolina, 23, 130
Greensboro College, 23
Greensboro Female College, 23
Greenwich, Connecticut, 107
Gregory, T. Watt, 30
Grimm, Jacob, xv
Grimm, Wilhelm, xv

H

Hadley, Arthur T., 24
Hadley, James, 24
Hamilton Debating Society, 60
Hampton, Wade, 12
Hardee, William J., 50
Hardin, John B., 45
Harkins, Thomas F., 100
"Harmony Hill" (Webb family home), 6–7
Harris, Mary Emma, 5, 85
Hart's Island, New York City (Union prison), 12
Harvard Law School, 66, 128
Harvard Summer School, 119
Harvard University, 5–6, 47, 65–66, 119
Hawaii, 65
Hazel Cemetery (Bell Buckle, TN), xviii, 61, 73, 88, 95, 98, 110–111, 117
Headmaster's Room, "Inn at Bingham School" (Oaks, NC), 8
Daily Herald (Columbia, Tennessee), 23
High Windy, Blue Ridge, North Carolina, 110
Highland Rim, 51
Highway 82, Tennessee (Sawney Webb Memorial Highway), 114
Highway 269 (Bedford County, TN), 117

INDEX

Highway 231, U.S., 114
Hill, Daniel H., 11
Hillsboro, North Carolina, 11
Hillsborough Academy, 7–8
Hinkle Hill (Bell Buckle, TN), 50, 115
History of Methodism in South Carolina (1883), 102
History of Vanderbilt University (1946), 31–32, 63
Holiday Inn, 109
Holidays, surprise, 38
Holliman, Glenn N., 4, 38–39, 56, 59, 71–72
Hollinger archival box (acid-free), xx
Homer, 96
Honor Code/System, xvi, 5, 70–71
Honorary degrees, 15–16, 18, 73, 75
Horace, 25
Horner, James H., 8
Horner (Classical) School, 8, 11–12, 19, 119
Horner Military School, 12
Howell, Susan Coop, xxi, 72
Hugo, 120
Humphrey, Willy, 31
Huntsville, Alabama, xviii, xix, xx, 72, 128

I

Inauguration, presidential, 1913 (Woodrow Wilson), 109
Independent Democrats, 56
Indian mysticism, 106
"Inn at Bingham School" (Oaks, NC), 8
International Shoe Company, 67
Italy, 107
Ivy League, 65

J

Jackson Dormitory, 72
Jackson, Mississippi, 107, 121
Jackson, Thomas J. "Stonewall," 11
Jacobs, Will Alf., 136
Jefferson, Thomas, 17
Jefferson Medical College, 33
Jesus, 121–122

"John, the Beloved," 6, 122 *See* John Maurice Webb
John Webb home (Culleoka, TN), 25, 114
John Webb home (Bell Buckle, TN), 5, 53–56, 58, 70, 77, 93–96, 100, 116, 118
John Webb Library, Webb School (Bell Buckle, TN), xxi, 44–45, 72, 108
John Webb Library Award, 109
John M. Webb Library (Trinity College), 100–102
Johnson's Island, Ohio (Union prison), 14
Jones, Clara Louise (Mrs. Albert M. Webb), 108
"Jungle Farm," 104–105
Junior Room (Sawney Webb's classroom), xviii, xix, 34–37, 39–43, 45, 53, 58, 81, 116, 131–133
Junior Room, 1976 restoration, 39, 42
Jurisprudence, 83

K

Kenan professorships, UNC, 16
Kentucky, 15, 32
Key, Benjamin Witt, 94, 107
Key, Mrs. Benjamin Witt (Sarah Webb, John Webb family), 94, 107
Kirkland, James H., 56, 66, 77, 89, 95–97
Kissinger, Henry, 6, 119
Klein, Mike, 132
Knoxville, Tennessee, 75, 109

L

Lane's Latin Grammar, 44
Lanier, Sidney, 63
Lanson, Gustave, 103
Last Supper (Jesus), 121–122
Latin, 7, 9–10, 13, 26, 34, 37, 43, 51, 71, 82, 85, 101, 119, 127
Latino, 72
League of Nations, 67
Leak-Wall Papers, Southern Historical Collection, UNC, 20
Lee, Robert E., 14, 17–18, 51
Letterheads, 46, 59, 135

Lewisburg, Tennessee, 69
Liars Club (Vanderbilt University), 32
Liberal Christianity, 76
Liberty Gap (1863), 51
Library of Congress, 132
Library of Congress card system, 44
Library of Congress classification system, 101
Liddell, St. John R., 50–51
Lincoln, Abraham, 11
Literary Digest (1913), 109
Little, Hannah (Byrd), xxi
Louisiana, 85
Louisville, Kentucky, 16, 28, 32
Louisville Courier Journal, 15
Louisville Times, 15
Louvin Brothers, 115
Louvin, Charlie, 115–116
Louvin, Ira, 115
Lynch [House] Hotel (Bell Buckle, TN), 50, 53, 57, 115
Lynchburg, Virginia, 66, 73, 108
Lytle, Andrew, 63, 109
Lytle, Thomas B., 30

M

Maccallum, May, 20
MacDonald, George, 53, 56
Main Street (Webb Road) (Bell Buckle, TN), xviii, 36, 40, 43, 57, 95, 115, 131
Malvern Hill, Virginia, 11
Manning, John Jr., 61–62
Mantra, 56
Maple Street (Bell Buckle, TN), xx, 56–58, 95, 100, 116, 132
Maplewood Cemetery, Section 12, (Durham, NC), 100
Marion, Alabama, xx
Marion Military Institute, xx
Marion Military Institute (MMI) Foundation, xx
Marlboro County, South Carolina, 103
Marquis Who's Who in America, 65
Maryland, 106
Masonic Lodge (Culleoka, TN), 113
Masons, 15, 113

Massachusetts, 67
Massey School, 69
Mathematics, 7, 9, 13, 26, 28, 71, 82, 85, 127
Maury County, Tennessee, 21–22, 29, 112
Maury County, 1880 Census, 27
Maury County Public Schools, 30
Maxwell House (Nashville, TN), 70
McCarley, Theodore T., 128
McCombs, William F. (Frank), 67
McCurtain, Chief [Edmund?], 28
McLean, Emma (Webb), 6, 18, 61
McLean, Dugald (McDugald) K., 69, 128, 135–136
McMillin, Laurence, xvii, 5–6, 51, 68, 107
McMillin, Mr. and Mrs., 29, 54, 56
McMinnville, Tennessee, 59, 115
McQuiddy, David N., 44
McTyeire, Holland N., 24, 32, 66, 95
Mebanesville (Mebane Station), North Carolina, 7, 10, 129–130
Mebane, North Carolina, 7, 15, 129–130
Mebane City Cemetery, North Carolina, 10
Memorial Hall, UNC, 15
Memphis, Tennessee, 99
Methodist Church (Culleoka, TN), 21–22, 25, 28, 64, 112–114, 132
Methodist Episcopal [M.E.] Church, South (Bell Buckle, TN), 58–59, 116
Methodists, 24, 27, 47, 66, 78, 102, 125
Mexicans, 26, 72
Michigan, viii, 55
Middle Tennessee, 51, 113–114
Middle Tennessee State University (MTSU), 132
Miller, Richard, viii
Ministerial students, 8, 26, 30
Mims, Edwin, 6, 12–13, 31–32, 60, 63, 76–78, 82, 88–90, 95, 121–122, 135
Mims Hall, Vanderbilt University, 63
Mims, Stewart L., 34, 87, 94

INDEX

Mims, Mrs. Stewart L. (Mary Gillespie Webb, John Webb family), 87, 94, 107
Mississippi, 27–28, 66, 121
Mobile, Alabama, 51
Modernism, 76
Monteagle, Tennessee, 78–79, 116
Monteagle Assembly, 78–79
Monteagle Sunday School Assembly, 78–79
Moore Institute (Culleoka, TN), 30
Moore, Merrill, 63
Morgan School, 69
"Morning talk" (Sawney Webb, Big Room), 37
Morrison, Robert Hall, 11
Mount Repose, North Carolina, 8, 11
Mount Tirzah, North Carolina, 7
Mullins family (Bell Buckle, TN), 54–55
Mullins, James D., 55
Murfreesboro, Tennessee, 49, 55, 77, 82, 95, 114
Murray, H.G., 70
Muse, A. W., house (Bomar) (Bell Buckle, TN), 83, 114–115

N

Namozine Church, Virginia, 11
Nance, Walter, 66
"Napoleon of schoolmasters," 8 *See* William James Bingham
Nashville, Tennessee, 24, 26, 29–31, 49, 59, 69, 73, 76–78, 87, 94–95, 98, 108, 114
Nashville & Chattanooga Railroad, 29, 49–50
Nashville, Chattanooga & St. Louis Railway, 49, 95
Nashville and Decatur Railroad, 22
Nashville Banner, 70
Nashville Teachers' Association, 70
Nashville Tennessean and The Nashville American, 93, 97
National Democratic Party, 67
National Education Association (NEA), 15, 32

National Register of Historic Places, 8, 42, 45, 113, 116
National Trust Project, 8
The Natural Bent (1949), 11
Negroes, 58
New England preparatory schools, 107
New Haven, Connecticut, 94
New Jersey, 4, 5, 70
New Orleans, Louisiana, 76, 84
New Testament (Greek), 118
New York, 78, 128
New York City, New York, 12, 94, 107, 131
Nicodemus, 121
"Nishtha" (Margaret Woodrow Wilson), 106
Normandy, Tennessee, 114
North Carolina, xvi, xix, 7, 8, 11, 15, 21, 29, 31, 56, 61, 69
North Carolina General Assembly, 9
North Carolina National Guard, 14
North Carolina Railroad, 10
North Carolina Third Battalion Light Artillery (Company A), CSA, 129–130
Northampton County, North Carolina, 130

O

"O Love That Wilt Not Let Me Go," 95
Oaks, North Carolina, 4, 6–12, 14, 17–18
Ohio, 12
"Old Jack," 5, 35, 90, 98, 120 *See* John Maurice Webb
"Old Johnny," xxvii, 5, 80, 88–89, 92, 98, 119 *See* John Maurice Webb
"Old Sawney," 32, 46, 67, 81, 90, 99 *See* William Robert Webb (Sawney)
"Old Sawney's," 4, 67 *See* Webb School (Bell Buckle, TN)
"Old Sawney's" (*The Atlantic Monthly*, 1920), 4, 81
"Old Sawney's: A Portrait of Webb School, 1870–1930," xix
Old Virginia, 6
"Opposites," xvii, xxviii, 19, 121
The Oracle (Webb School newspaper), 43
Orange County, North Carolina, 6, 12

Oregon, 68
Origin of Species, 44
Ottley, Charles W., 70
Oxford, Mississippi, 76
Oxford, North Carolina, 8, 12, 19
Oxford University, xviii, 4–5, 64, 83, 85–86, 119, 127–128

P

Paducah, Kentucky, 63
Page, Walter Hines, 8
Paine, Robert, 27–28
"Painted lady" (Queen Anne style), 53
Palm Sunday, 14
Paris, France, 103, 119
Paris Peace Conference (Versailles Conference) (1919), 67
The Parthenon, 75
Paschall, Annie, 68
Paty house (Bell Buckle, TN), 83, 114
Paty, Raymond R., 66
Peabody Institute of Music, 106
Pennsylvania, 65, 84
Peoples, R. Grier, 61, 135
Peoples-Tucker School, 69
People's Bank and Trust Co. (Bell Buckle, TN), 57, 115
PPE (Philosophy, Politics, and Economics), Oxford University, 119
Pericles, 121
Peroration (Daniel Webster, Dartmouth College case, 1818), 121
Person County, North Carolina, 6–8
Peru, 66
Petersburg, Virginia (prisoner exchange), 12
Peyton (president, Nashville, Chattanooga & St. Louis Railway), 95
Ph.D. degree, 127
Phi Beta Kappa, 15, 44, 61, 65, 73, 87, 128
Philadelphia, Pennsylvania, 65
Phillips, Billy, 115
Phillips Academy, 61, 67, 107

Phillips General Store (Bell Buckle, TN), 115
Phinizy, Bowdre, 28–29, 44, 46–48
Picerno, Nicholas P., 130
Pied Piper, xvi
Piedmont region, North Carolina, 8
Pittsboro, North Carolina, 11
Pittsborough Academy, 8
Plato, 121
Plato's Academy, 121
Platonic Debating Society, Webb School, (Bell Buckle, TN), 47, 60
Platonic Debating Society Room (Junior Room), 45
Platonic Society (Public Secretary), Webb School (Bell Buckle, TN), 47
Pleasant Grove Station (Culleoka, TN), 21–22
Poet Laureate of Tennessee, xvi, xix, 115
Point Lookout, Maryland (prisoner exchange), 14
Pondicherry, India, 106
Portability, 9, 11, 28–29, 35, 45
Porter, Earl, 102
Post-Reconstruction South, 3
Poteat, Edwin McNeill Memorial Gates, 43
Poynter, Horace, 67
Presbyterians, 10, 15
"President's Room" (Princeton University), 4, 69
Presidents, U.S., xvi, 4–5, 48, 119
Price, Edward T. (Ed), 59, 69, 135–136
Price, Susan (Webb) (Mrs. Edward T. Price), 69
Price-Webb School, 69
Prince Harry of Wales, 61
Prince William of Cambridge, 61
Princeton, New Jersey, 4–5, 70
"Princeton System," 4, 70
Princeton University, xvi, xviii, 4–5, 46, 56, 65–67, 69–70, 82
Princeton University, The Graduate Council, 5, 70
Princeton University, Honor System, xvi, 4–5, 70

INDEX

Principals, Webb School (Bell Buckle), xxviii, 3, 11, 38
"Private conference," Tennessee educators (1911), 89
"Proceedings of the Sixth Meeting…" (SACS), 75–76, 125
Proctor, Robert, 135
Prohibition, 22, 109
Pulitzer Prize, xvi, 4, 42, 64, 68, 109
Puryear Building, The Webb School (Bell Buckle, TN), 45
Puryear, Clara (Mrs. Edwin Mims), 63

Q

Quakers, 84
Queen Anne style, 53
Query Club (Nashville, TN), 77

R

Racism, 6, 22, 27, 71–72
Rail Road Square (Bell Buckle, TN), 131
Raleigh, North Carolina, 100, 107
Raleigh News & Observer, 100, 107
Rand, Frank C., 67
Rand, Henry, 67
Rand Dormitory (Cafeteria), xix, xx, 67, 72
Randolph College, 73
Randolph School, xviii
Randolph-Macon College for Women, 66, 68, 91
Randolph-Macon Woman's College, 66, 68, 73
Ransom, John Crowe, 63
RC Cola & Moon Pie Festival (Bell Buckle, TN), 116
Reconstruction, 18, 21, 72
Red Cross, American, 67, 106
Responsions, Oxford University, 119, 127
Reuel B. Pritchett Museum (Bridgewater College), xx
Reynolds, Katherine (Chaddock), 127
Rhodes Scholars, xviii, 4, 64, 66, 83, 85, 121, 127–128
Rhodes Scholars, wall listing, The Webb School (Bell Buckle, TN), 116

Rhodes Scholarships, xvi, xviii, 3–4, 6, 64–66, 69, 83, 85, 127–128
Rhodes Trust, Oxford University, 83
Rice, John Andrew, xvi, 5, 35, 39, 42–43, 66, 71, 81, 83–87, 90–92, 97–98, 115, 128–129
Rice, John Andrew II, 84
Rice, Nell Aydelotte, 83–84, 98
Richardson, J.H., 23
Richardson, Lynn, 107
Richmond County, North Carolina, 19–20
Richmond County Historical Society, 20
Richmond, Virginia, 51
Riverside Cemetery (Asheville, NC), 15
Rock Island, Tennessee, 59
Rockefeller, John D., 16
Rockingham, North Carolina, 19–20, 23
Rockingham Sabbath School, 19–20
Roman style, 57
Roosevelt, Theodore, 70
Rose Hill Plantation (Marlboro County, SC), 103
Rosecrans, William S., 51
Ross, George T., 128
Royster, Vermont, 4, 42, 68
Ryman Auditorium, 30

S

Salem Academy, 110, 115
Salem Cemetery (Bell Buckle, TN), 110
Saloons, 22–23, 25, 29 *See also* Alcohol and Prohibition
San Francisco, California, 81
Sanborn Fire Map, Culleoka, TN, 112
Sanborn Map Company, 131–132
Sanborn-Perris Fire Insurance Maps, Bell Buckle, TN, 52, 112, 131–132
Sanders, Albert G., 29, 54–56, 58, 107, 121, 128
Sanders, Shipp, 107
Sanger Clinic, 68
Sanger Heart and Vascular Institute, 68
Sanger, Paul W., 68
Sanitarium, 61
Sanskrit, 118–119
Sawney Hall, 58, 116

Sawney Webb barn (Bell Buckle, TN), 116
Sawney Webb Big Room (Bell Buckle, TN), 36
Sawney Webb farm (Culleoka, TN), 24
Sawney Webb farm (Bell Buckle, TN), 116
Sawney Webb Hall, 58, 116
Sawney Webb home (Bell Buckle, TN), 53, 57–58, 116
Sawney Webb home (Culleoka, TN), 22
Sawney Webb Memorial Highway (Tennessee Highway 82), 114
"School Libraries" (John Maurice Webb), 75, 123–125
Schoolhouse (Bell Buckle, TN) *See* Big Room
Schoolhouse (Culleoka, TN), 28
The Schoolmaker (1971), xviii, 5–6, 51, 68, 107, 120
Schools, portable, 9, 11, 28–29, 35, 45
Science Hill (Bell Buckle, TN), 114
Science Hill Academy, 83, 115
Mr. Scruggs (Bell Buckle, TN), 114
Sea Girt, New Jersey, 67
Second North Carolina Cavalry (Company K), CSA, 12
Secretary of State, U.S., 6, 119
"Select Classical and Mathematical School," 9 *See also* Bingham School (Oaks, NC)
Senate, U.S., 109
Senator, U.S., 4, 30, 88, 109, 119
Senior Hall (Senior Room), 81
Senior Room (John Webb's classroom and library), xix, 3, 5, 34, 37, 39–44, 53, 58, 71, 81–82, 86, 120, 131–133
"Servants" (slaves), 6, 72
Seventy-fifth Anniversary, Webb School, Bell Buckle, TN (1946), 6, 121–122
Sewanee, Tennessee, 56, 65, 100, 109
Shakespeare, William, 96, 98, 120
Shelbyville, Tennessee, 49, 51, 66, 78, 114
Shelbyville Times-Gazette, 95, 98
Shipp, Albert Micajah, 25, 102–103, 107

Shipp, Albert M. (son of Albert Micajah Shipp), 107
Shipp, Mary Jane (Gillespie) (Mrs. Albert Micajah Shipp), 25, 95, 103
Shipp, S.W.G., 107
Shipp, Susie V., 103, 107
Shipp, Thornwell T., 55, 107
Shofner, H.B., 136
Simpson, J. Russell, 44
"Sister Lillie," 104
Slave owners, 6
Slavery, 6, 72
Smallpox, 83
Smiser, James A., 30
Snead (Sneed), Edward D., 130
Snead's Company, Local Defense militia (North Carolina), 130
Socrates, 27, 121
"Son Will." *See* William Robert Webb Jr.
Son Will Building, xix, 45, 62, 72, 116
Son Will home (Bell Buckle, TN), 43
Soochow University, China, 66
Sorbonne, Paris, France, 107, 119
The South, xviii, 3–4, 8–9, 15, 18, 22, 24, 32, 63, 74, 88, 95, 101, 106
South Anna Bridge, Virginia, 14
South Atlantic Quarterly (Duke University), 63
South Carolina, xix
Southern Association of Colleges and Schools (SACS), 63, 73, 75–76, 89
Southern Historical Collection, UNC, 20, 26, 28–29, 46
Southern Living magazine, xviii
Southerners, 15, 26, 56
Spartan, 61
Spartansburg, South Carolina, 73, 103
Spica, setter (John Webb family dog), 55
Split-bottom chairs, 37, 81
Sports, 40, 45, 55, 60
Sri Aurobindo Ashram, 106
Stainback, Ingram M., 65
Stanbury, W.A., 107
Standard Oil Company, 16

INDEX 157

State historical marker, The Webb
    School (Bell Buckle, TN),
    116–117
Stephenson, C.D., 136
Stile, 37
Stock Market Crash (1929), 57
Stokes, Walter Jr., 120
Stoneman, George, 10
Stoneman's Raid, 9–10
"Stony Point" (Webb family home),
    (Oaks, NC), 6, 7, 9, 12
Stuart, James Ewell Brown (J.E.B.), 12
Stuart, Jesse, 63
Student Center, The Webb School (Bell
    Buckle, TN), 45
Student retention, 71
Study hall, outdoor, 37
"Suggestions For Beginning A School
    Library" (John Maurice Webb),
    75, 123–125
Sulphur water, 46
Summer School/Camp, 59
The Sunday School Magazine (1927), 27
Swarthmore College, 83–84
Sweetwater, Tennessee, 44
Sycamore Retreat (The Batch), 24
Sydney, Saint Bernard (Sawney Webb
    family dog), 55

T

Taft, Horace, 65
Taft School, 65
Tapeworm, 33
Tar Heel State, *See* North Carolina
Tate, Allen, 63, 109
Taylor, Peter, 109
Taylor, Robert Love, 48, 109
Tennessee, xix, 3–4, 11, 21–22, 30, 48,
    66, 68, 95
Tennessee Backroads, 116
Tennessee Centennial and International
    Exposition (Nashville, TN), 75
Tennessee Historical Commission, 39,
    42, 45, 113
Tennessee Historical Quarterly, 4, 56
Tennessee House of Representatives, 66
Tennessee Military Institute, 44

Tennessee Philological Association
    (1905), 78
Tennessee state historical marker, The
    Webb School (Bell Buckle, TN),
    116–117
Tennessee state legislature, 109
Tennessee Valley Authority (TVA), 66
Tennessee Walking Horse, 114
Tennyson, 60, 96
Tenpenny Hill, 114
Texas, 30, 69
Thames River, 61
Thanksgiving, 48
Third Battalion (Light Artillery), North
    Carolina (Company A), CSA,
    129–130
Thompson Hall, 37
Tigert, John J., 66, 128
Tillett, Wilbur F., 95, 119
Towson, Hatton D., 128
Trapping, 28–29, 38
Tree City USA, 116
Trinity and Duke, 1892–1924 (1964),
    102
Trinity College (Duke University), 63,
    88–89, 94–95, 100–101, 103, 107
Trinity College Library, 100–103
Tuberculosis, 69
Tullahoma, Tennessee, 114
Tullahoma Campaign (1863), 50–51
Tulane University, 84–85
Typhoid fever, 68

U

Ulysses, 82
Uncle Remus, 59
Undersecretary of State, U.S., 67
Union Army, 51
"Union" barrier (John Maurice Webb),
    90
Union Station (Nashville, TN), 78
Unionville, Tennessee, 23
U.S. Army, 15
University Cemetery (Sewanee, TN),
    109
University of Alabama, 66, 128
University of Berlin, 73

University of Cambridge, 16
University of Chicago, 44, 65, 83, 98
University of Florida, 66
University of Georgia, 47, 75
University of Leipzig, 73
University of London, 16
University of Louisville, 15, 16
University of Madrid, 107
University of Mississippi, 65
University of Nashville, 75
University of North Carolina, 7–8, 11–12, 14–18, 20, 23, 25–26, 31, 46, 56, 61–63, 65–66, 87, 109, 129–130
University of Oxford, xviii, 4, 16, 127–128
University of Pennsylvania, 65
University of Tennessee, 65, 109, 132
The University of the South, 56, 65, 78, 100, 108–109, 128
University of the South Archives, 108–109
University of the South, Associated Alumni, 108
University of the South, Distinguished Faculty Award, 108
University of the South, Francis S. Houghteling, Professor of American History, 108
University of Texas, 65
University of Virginia, 15, 17, 65, 75
University System of Georgia, 66
Up From Slavery (1901), 56
Upper Duck River Watershed, 49
Uremia, 106

V

"The Vanderbilt," 31
Vanderbilt Commodores (football), 67
Vanderbilt University, 3, 5–6, 25, 31–32, 44, 56, 63, 65–66, 68–69, 73, 75, 88–89, 90, 95–97, 103, 119, 135
Vanderbilt University, Board of Trust, 32, 66–67
Vanderbilt University, English Department, 6, 63
Vanderbilt University, Humanities Division, 63

Vassar College, 68
Vaughn, Margaret (Britton) "Maggi," xv, xvi, xix, xx, 115
Venable, Francis, 56, 61–62
Venable, Sally (Charleton) Manning (Mrs. Francis Venable), 61
Versailles Conference (Paris Peace Conference) (1919), 67
Victorian style, 53, 57
Virgil, 77, 96
Virginia, xx, 11–12, 14, 31, 73, 109
Visions and Vanities: John Andrew Rice of Black Mountain College (1998), 127

W

W.J. Bingham and Sons (Oaks, NC), 14
W.J. Bingham's Select School. *See* Bingham School (Oaks, NC)
The Wall Street Journal, 4, 42
Wallace, South Carolina, 102–103
Walling, Tennessee, 59
Warren, Robert Penn, 63
Wartrace, Tennessee, 114, 117
Washington, Booker T., 56
Washington College (Washington & Lee University), 17–18, 65
Washington, D.C., 88, 109
Watkins, Elton, 68
Watkins Hall (Nashville, TN), 70
Watson, Tom, 109
"Webb" monument, Hazel Cemetery (Bell Buckle, TN), 98, 117
Webb, Adline (Addie), 23, 27
Webb, Albert Micajah (John Webb family), 25–27, 74, 87, 90, 93–94, 99–103, 107–108
Webb, Alexander Smith, 6–7, 17
Webb, Alla, 27, 44
Webb, Clara Louise (Jones) (Mrs. Albert M. Webb), 108
Webb, Clary, 93, 99
Webb, Cornelia (John Webb family), 25–27, 94, 100, 107–108
Webb, Cornelia Adeline (Stanford), 6–7, 17

INDEX

Webb, Ellen (Farnum) (Mrs. John M. Webb II), 109
Webb, Emma (Mrs. Dugald McLean), 69
Webb, Emma (Clary) (Mrs. Sawney Webb), 22–24, 27, 33, 55, 61, 87, 98
Webb Family Papers (Webb-Moore Papers), Southern Historical Collection, UNC, 12, 26
Webb Follin Administration Building and Chapel, xviii, 62
Webb, Hazel Alexander (John Webb family), 25, 98, 108, 110–111, 117
Webb, James H., 12
Webb, John (Sawney Webb family), 24, 27
Webb, John M. (Confederate artillery officer), 129–130
Webb, John Maurice
    Achievements, vxiii, 3–4, 120–122
    Birth and birthdate, 6
    Family and boyhood, 6–7
    First teacher, 6–7
    Wisdom bump, xxvii, 7, 97
    Civil War and student at Bingham School (Oaks, NC), 7–9
    Civil War and student at Bingham School (Mebanesville, NC), 7, 9–12
    Academic "star" at Bingham School, 12–13
    Service in the Confederacy, 129–130
    Desire to attend the University of Virginia, 17
    Student at the University of North Carolina, Chapel Hill, 17–18
    Dialectic Society, UNC, 18
    Academic degrees from UNC, 18
    Teacher at Bingham School (Mebanesville, NC), 18–19
    Principal and teacher in Rockingham, NC, 19–20
    Educational plans with brother Sawney, 19–20, 23
    Joins Sawney in Culleoka, TN, 23
    Culleoka Institute, 21–30
    Appearance and persona, xxviii, 23, 27, 96–98, 118, 122
    Humility of, 91, 97, 111
    "Opposites," xvii, xviii, 19, 21
    Teaching methods, 23–24, 27, 80–81
    Greek study during Cholera epidemic, 24
    Classroom in Culleoka, NC, 25
    Marriage to Lily Shipp in Nashville, TN, 24–25
    Welcome on Vanderbilt University campus, 25
    John and Lily's children, 25–26, 58, 107–108
    House in Culleoka, TN, 25, 114
    Co-Principal and partners with Sawney, xxviii, 3, 11, 23, 38
    Teaches Vanderbilt's best students, 31–32
    Culleoka Academy, 28–30
    Prohibitionist, 22, 29
    Runs school in Sawney's absence, 29, 60–61
    Illnesses, 18–19, 58, 61, 81, 93
    Move to Bell Buckle, TN, 29, 33–34
    Designs school buildings with Sawney, 34
    Opens Webb School with brother Sawney, 33–34
    House on Maple Street, 47, 53–56, 116
    Personal library, 54, 96, 100–102
    Senior Room (classroom and library), 34, 37, 39–45
    Library policies, 43–44
    Teaches Greek to juniors, 24
    Teaches all seniors, 71
    Racial matters and concerns, 6, 22, 56, 71–72
    Independent Democrat, 56
    Serving the Methodists, 58–59
    Mentor to children, 78
    Mentor to Edwin Mims, 6, 12, 60, 63
    Death of Hazel Webb, 98, 108, 110
    President of SACS, 75–76
    Detests "standardization" (Carnegie Units), 76, 85, 89

Decision to leave SACS, 76
Scholarship, 74–77
Educational philosophy and concerns, 88-90
Leisure activities, 55–56
Bicyclist, 56
Chautauqua, 78–79
President of the Bank of Bell Buckle, 56–57
President of Tennessee Philological Association (1905), 78
The Club (Dante Club), 77
Lectures widely, 77–78
Honorary doctorate, 75
Religious interests and concerns, 58–59, 76–77, 111
Rational thought, 77
"Union" barrier, 90
Success of alumni, 64–69
Dispute with Sawney and rupture between families, 86–88
Last illness and death, 92–93
Burial in Hazel Cemetery, 95–98, 117
Eulogized by Vanderbilt chancellor and others, 95–97
Unmarked grave, 98, 111, 117
Abandonment of Webb School and Bell Buckle by his family, 100
Lily Webb's bitterness towards Sawney and Son Will, 99–100, 104–107
Donation of John Webb's personal library to Trinity College, 100–103
Successes and sorrow of the extended John Webb family, 106–109
Tributes to John Webb, 118–122
"John, the Beloved," 6, 121, 122
Webb, John Maurice II, 100, 108–109
Webb, Lily (Shipp) (Mrs. John Maurice Webb), 24–25, 27, 55–57, 70, 72, 87–88, 95, 98–100, 102, 104–108, 111, 117
Webb, Louise (Hall) Manning (Mrs. W.R. Webb Jr.), 61, 98
Webb, Mary (Gillespie) (John Webb family), 25, 87, 107–108

Webb-Moore Papers (Webb Family Papers), Southern Historical Collection, UNC, 26
Webb Road (Main Street) (Bell Buckle, TN), 36, 43, 115
Webb, Samuel Henry, 6–7, 17–18
Webb, Sarah (John Webb family), 25, 107–108
Webb, Susan (Sawney Webb family), 69
Webb, Susan Ann "Suny," 6–7, 17–18, 28–29, 38
Webb, Thompson, 69, 86
Webb, William Alexander, 63, 66, 68, 73
Webb, William Robert "Sawney"
Achievements, xxviii, 3–4, 109–110
Birth, 7
Nicknamed "Sawney," 7
Family and boyhood, 6–7
First teacher, 6–7
Student at Hillsborough Academy, 7
Student at Bingham School (Oaks, NC), 7–8
Student at the University of North Carolina, Chapel Hill, 7, 11–12
Academic degrees from UNC, 12
Service in the Confederacy, 10–12
Wounded at Malvern Hill, 11
Teaching stints at Horner (Classical) School, 11–12
Captured at Amelia Courthouse, Virginia, 12
Imprisoned at Hart's Island, New York City, 12
New York City sojourn, 12
Works to send brother John to UNC, 17–18
Works to send brother Sam to Washington College, 17–18
Decision to move to Tennessee, 20–21
Educational plans with brother John, 19–20, 23
Secures teaching position in Culleoka, TN, 21
Culleoka Institute, 21–30
Appearance and persona, xxviii, 23–29, 109–110
Educational views, 23–24, 27, 44

INDEX

Teaching methods (Trapping), 28–29, 38
"Webb's School," 26
House in Culleoka, 24–25, 113
The Batch, 24, 113
Curriculum and boarding rules, 26–27
Joined by brother John, 23
Co-Principal and partners with John, xxviii, 3, 11, 23, 38
Cholera epidemic, 24
Marries Emma Clary in Unionville, TN, 23
Sawney and Emma's children, 24
Shares home with brother John and Lily, 25
Culleoka Academy, 28–30
Teaches Vanderbilt's best students, 31–32
Speech to NEA, 32
Prohibitionist, 22, 29, 109
Makes enemies, 29, 71, 86
Contracts tapeworm, 33–34
Fist fights and nearly beaten to death, 29, 58
Recuperation from injuries, 29
Decision to move to Bell Buckle, TN, 29, 33-34
Designs school buildings with brother John, 34
Opens Webb School with brother John, 33–34
Junior Room (Sawney's classroom), 34, 37, 39–42, 45
Big Room "morning talks," 37
"Opposites," xvii, xxviii, 19, 21
Curriculum matters, 37, 51, 85, 117
Rules and regulations, 26–27, 37, 51
Boarding house system, 9, 12, 22, 24, 26–27, 37, 46, 72
Discipline and corporal punishment, 35, 38
Success of alumni, 64–69
Declines presidency of the University of Tennessee, 109
Minority recruiting, 26, 71–72
Racial attitudes, 6, 22, 27, 71–72
Eulogizes Edward Carmack, 30

Illnesses, 87–88, 110
Detests Carnegie Units (SACS), 76, 85, 89
Dispute with John M. Webb family, 86–88
Leaves Son Will in charge of Webb School, 87–88
U.S. Senator, 88, 109
Flag bill, 109
Speech to U.S. Senate, 109
Webb family rupture upon John Webb's death, 99–100
Honorary doctorates, 109
Travel, 110
Last illness and death, 110
Burial in Hazel Cemetery (marked grave), 110
Honors and tributes, xxviii, 3–4, 109–110
Webb Tower's "grief," 110
Webb, William Robert Jr. (Son Will), xix, 24, 27, 34, 43–44, 56, 60–62, 76, 82, 86–88, 98, 135–136
Webb, William Robert "Bob" III, 69
Webb & Company, 19
Webb Old Boys, 4–6, 32
Webb Old Girls, 4
"Webb Rhodes Scholar," xviii, 5–6, 127–128
Webb School (Bell Buckle, TN), xv, xvi
Webb School (Knoxville, TN), 69
Webb School, Alumni Association (Bell Buckle, TN), 72, 109
Webb School Archives (Bell Buckle, TN), xix, xx, xxi, 27, 43, 45, 114
Webb School Arts and Crafts Fair (Bell Buckle, TN), 116
Webb School, Board of Trustees (Bell Buckle, TN), 62, 72, 88, 108
Webb School, Honor Code/System, xvi, 5, 70–71
"The Webb School Junior Room, The Symbol of a School" (1977), 4, 56
Webb School Orchestra, 60
Webb Summer School (Camp), 59
Webb School, Summer School program (1975), 59

Webb Schools (Claremont, California), 69
Webb Tower, 110
"Webb's School," 131, 133
Webster, Daniel, 121
Westmoreland, Ella B., 27
Whipping (corporal punishment), 35, 38
"Whipping rooms" (Big Room), 35, 38
White, William Webb, 128
Whiteside, Annie, 91
Whiteside, F.W., 135
Whiteside, Henry O., 68
Whiteside, Mabel Kate, 68, 91
Who's Who in America, 6, 65
Wiggins, Benjamin, 56
Wilcox, R.B., 12
Wiley, Tommy L., 115
Wilkesboro, North Carolina, 23
William Bond Library, The Webb School (Bell Buckle, TN), xx, 3, 108–109
Wilmington, North Carolina, 8, 11
Wilson, Ellen Louise (Axson), 106
Wilson, J.R., Mr. and Mrs., 70
Wilson, Margaret Woodrow, 56, 106
Wilson, Matthew, 109
Wilson, Woodrow, xviii, 4, 30, 56, 67, 69–70, 106, 109
Windsor Castle, 61
Wisdom bump, xxvii, 7, 97
Wofford College, 73, 103
Wolf Pit (Richmond County, North Carolina), 20
Woodlawn Memorial Park (Nashville, TN), 63
Wordsworth, 60
World War I, 8, 52, 83, 91, 106, 109
World War II, 57, 112
Wright, Fielding Lewis, 65–66
Wyatt, Inzer B., 128

Y

Yale University, 24, 65, 74, 107–108
Yancey, Benjamin Cudworth, 48
Young Men's Christian Association (YMCA), 59

ABOUT THE AUTHOR

Terry Barkley is an independent scholar and musician who lives in Monteagle, Tennessee. He retired in 2012 as director of the Brethren Historical Library and Archives at the Church of the Brethren General Offices in Elgin, Illinois. He previously served as MMI Foundation archivist in the Baer Memorial Library at Marion Military Institute in Marion, Alabama.

Terry is listed in Who's Who in the World, Who's Who in America, Who's Who in American Education, Directory of American Scholars, and in the Alabama Music Hall of Fame. He is also the author of *One Who Served: Brethren Elder Charles Nesselrodt of Shenandoah County, Virginia* (3rd edition, Lot's Wife Publishing, 2004).

CPSIA information can be obtained at www.ICGtesting.com
Printed in the USA
LVOW04s0709170415

434843LV00002BA/3/P